Socha
Bhi Na
Tha

Socha Bhi Na Tha

SRIMAN NARAYANAN

Srishti
PUBLISHERS & DISTRIBUTORS

SRISHTI PUBLISHERS & DISTRIBUTORS
Registered Office: N-16, C.R. Park
New Delhi – 110 019
Corporate Office: 212A, Peacock Lane
Shahpur Jat, New Delhi – 110 049
editorial@srishtipublishers.com

First published by
Srishti Publishers & Distributors in 2019

Copyright © Sriman Narayanan, 2019

10 9 8 7 6 5 4 3 2 1

Printed at Repro Knowledgecast Limited, Thane

Krishnarpanam

Yat-karosai yad-asnasi yaj-juhosi-dadasi yat,
Yat tapasyasi kaunteya tat kurusva mad-arpanam

(*Bhagavad Gita*, chapter 9, verse 27)

Whatever you do, whatever you eat, whatever you offer as oblation to the sacred fire, whatever you give away as charity, whatever austerity you perform, O son of Kunti, do it as an offering to Me.

Jai Guru Dev

Salutations

Mukam karoti vaacaalam pangum langhayate girim,
Yat-krpaatamaham vande param-aananda madhavam.

(*Bhagavad Gita, Gita Dhyanam*, verse 8)

✳

I salute that Madhava, the source of Supreme Bliss,
Whose grace renders the dumb man eloquent,
And the cripple cross mountains.

Hari Om

"Gahana Karmano Gathih"

Unfathomable are the ways of Karma[*]

(*Bhagavad Gita,* chapter 4, verse 17)

This book is about two women in the protagonist's life. One, whose love he had, and whom he had loved and wanted to marry; and the other for whom he had no love and did not want to marry.

"Life is what happens to you, when you are busy making other plans."

"The mills of god grind slow; But, they grind exceedingly fine."

---

[*] The way in which the results of our actions *(karma)* manifest is beyond comprehension. Some may come in this lifetime, or in the next, or in a distant future lifetime.

Confession by the author

This is no literary work, and hence, is not bound to provide the intellect with eloquence, waxed with superior sounding words, or charm the mind with a bombast of poetic prose.

It's a fictional story, straight from the heart, written in simple English. It is about life, love and marriage, narrated with spiritual reflections, and I believe you shall find it to be an entertaining, suspenseful, contemplative and insightful read.

Confession of the protagonist

I wrote the initial thirteen chapters several years ago, as I had a huge urge to have a book published. Although the possibility of such an occurrence was a long shot, as in one in a million kind of thing, bordering on never. Yet I held on to that fantasy, primarily as the only way that I could think about redeeming myself with Aditi. I had the intention of e-mailing the link to the book to her, and making her aware about all that I had wanted to say; which I did not and could not back then.

My vain hope was that if she was still tormented by my actions, as to why I did what I did so abruptly without any fore-warning, my telling her the complete story, might aid her to get some closure. While I find my closure as well in the process, and lighten the burden of my guilt, knowing that I had at least relayed to her the reasons that I owed her. Otherwise, what kind of a person would just vanish without explaining the act of disappearance, leaving behind a broken heart, an incapacitated mind, a wounded soul.

However, when I received the final email from Aditi in 2005, I paused my writing; my core purpose was satisfied reading her response.

However, I resumed writing in the recent years, with a change in my original intent and motivation.

No longer driven by that primary urge to redeem myself, but just a strong desire to tell the story as it happened, and as I perceived it then.

I make no claims that I was right in all that I did. I have made many mistakes in life, and you may find me stupid, foolish, weak, bad, disgusting, strong, honest, emotional, thoughtful, cold hearted, or uncaring as you read through my story.

Any events or occurrences elicit multiple perspectives and viewpoints from people. The two women may have their own take on the events I narrate; or a very divergent perspective; but since it is I who is writing, it is my own view of what I perceived of my reality.

Shyam Venkat

1.1

1 June 2003

"You are such a heartless person. How can you do this? You have destroyed my life. You will never find any peace or happiness!" she screamed at me. "Do you think I will ever live after this? I will commit suicide. I loved you, and still love you. But you are the cruelest creature that I have ever seen in my life."

I looked at her, trembling with mixed emotions. I remained quiet. I wanted to leave the apartment, and reached for the door. But she pushed me with violent force, blocking the door and yelling hysterically, "Don't you even have a shred of compassion? A drop of kindness, or affection? Don't be silent. *Speak up now! Speakkk! Say something.* I will not let you ruin me. *I will not let you destroy my life!*"

I was still trembling, with my heart pounding heavily. I managed to reach the door when she moved away from it for a brief second, and left the apartment with my wallet and car keys.

2.1

I grew up in Coimbatore, the second biggest city in the state of Tamil Nadu. A city dotted with numerous educational institutions, textile mills, and textile machinery. It was often referred to as the Manchester of South India, due to the abundance of textile mills and surrounding cotton fields.

There was nothing noteworthy about me during my teens to talk about; I was a nerd then. My only focus was to excel in studies, and I was obsessed about securing the first rank in the examinations. I was the blue-eyed boy of my teachers and much loved, for that very reason.

I don't feel great about it as I reflect upon it now, that I had taken life so seriously and missed out on other aspects of fun and learning that life offered, like pursuing a sport, or learning an art.

However, a spark of glamour I discovered in myself during my seventh grade was ability to excel in public speaking.

A circular was received in the class, and it was read aloud by Mrs Rachel, my English teacher. There was an elocution contest to be hosted by the school in three weeks and participation was invited from all students. There was a sudden and an abrupt gush of desire in me to participate in the competition.

That evening, I told Radhika, my sister who studied in the same school in the tenth grade, about it.

The title of the elocution contest for the sixth to eighth graders was 'My happiest moment in life'.

Radhika gave me ideas and she helped me draft the speech. I practiced it numerous times.

On the day of the competition, the entire school was seated in the gallery section, located at the far end of the vast auditorium, on the rows of barren cement seats, each elevated over the other, facing the lectern and the tall floor mike. The row of seated students was interspersed briefly at varying spots by bold green aluminum chairs where the class teachers of different class-sections sat.

The elocution contest commenced grade-wise. When my turn came and I was called in to speak, Radhika felt her heart race. It was my first public speaking, and she became nervous and closed her eyes.

I rose from my seat and walked confidently to the lectern. I gave a quick glance at the sea of students assembled in front of me, and started my speech.

I spoke about my early evening walk one day, and how I was captivated by nature's beauty and became spell-bound by the dozen daffodils dancing and swaying to the tune and rhythm of the breeze. I said that was the happiest moment in my life.

I had never seen a daffodil before, but this was a story, invented just for the speech.

I spoke loud and clear, with natural confidence. It was easy as I had rehearsed it several times. As I finished, there was thunderous applause. I bagged the first prize.

That incident marked the beginning of my new-found passion. I started to participate in more competitions in the next few years at my school and others. My parents, teachers, family members, and friends' parents greatly appreciated my public speaking skills.

But there is something about my speaking skills that would surface years later, and change my life. Change it completely.

Unfathomable. *Socha bhi na tha.*

1.2

I got into my silver-grey Toyota Corolla and started to drive aimlessly. I felt lonely and vulnerable. I was seething with anger, accompanied by fear, pain and sadness. I wanted to get away from her.

It was 11 a.m. pacific time in San Diego. I wanted to call my mother and sister and tell them what had just happened. But India was more than eight hours ahead. It was past midnight there. So, I decided to write a long email to both, narrating the day's incident.

I drove to the nearest cyber café, which was the silent window to the world that was far away from me now.

As I opened my yahoo mailbox, a familiar vintage e-mail from three years ago from Shambhavi, whom I had met online, caught my attention. I had carefully preserved it in a separate folder.

28 May, 2000

Hello Shyam,

You say things which any woman would like. Is it all planned? Do you do it on purpose or are you that good?

I am doing 7a.m.–4 p.m. shifts these days. I have a funny idea and I know you wouldn't fall for it. But it seems so very interesting/romantic. I board one of the company Sumos for home at about 4 p.m. Would you come over and maybe we could try to recognize each other (a longshot, is it?). So, Thursday, Friday? Or perhaps it would be rather inconvenient. Do let me know.

Luv,
Shambhavi

That was Shambhavi's reply to the email that I had written to her, when our discussion drifted to life, love and marriage. Numerous times, when I had cleaned up my mail box in the past, I had always resisted deleting this email from Shambhavi.

I held on to her email, simply because her reply evoked images of a melancholic voice, a distressed heart betrayed by someone in her past. I had replayed her first two lines several times in my mind, contemplating the deeper personal emotion embedded in them. I wondered how cruel those men must be to betray someone's love, respect and trust.

I lowered my eyes and looked at the date the mail was sent. It was May 2000. Three years ago.

Shambhavi was just a little more than a friendly acquaintance, whom I had met online at Rediff Dating. We had kept in touch regularly over mails for a while, but then had lost touch over the years.

Today, when I read the same email after so long, my focus for the very first time shifted from her reply to my own.

For those words of mine served as a grim remainder of a painful irony that marked my life, and the unexpected twists and turns that followed.

27 May, 2000

Dear Shambhavi,

Glad to know that your day was good and you are having fun. I suppose women in general look for security, intelligence, humour and complete love. Men on the other hand look for looks, intelligence, humour and complete love, don't they? Until a few months, I had never given a deep thought about love.

I was just focused on my career and always believed that if it is meant to happen, it just happens. But now, I realize it doesn't happen like a fairy tale or love at first sight. What I mean is that one has to put some conscious effort in understanding the other person and to reach out for the vibes. It slowly evolves after that. My thoughts on these may sound very amateurish, but that's how I feel. I am in no hurry for marriage, but I want to find my girl.

After all, it's just one life and it's a partnership for a lifetime. Wouldn't it be nice if we could choose the relationship?

You agree?
Shyam

The pain and sadness in me amplified as I read the last line. How prophetic the words of mine were, if anything, but the contrary to what I wrote. An oxymoron.

The flood of emotions overwhelmed me and I collapsed on the table.

2.2

My dad was a professor and taught in the local government arts college in Coimbatore, and my mother ran a small nursery school behind our house. Dad had finished his Ph.D. in History at Sagar University, Madhya Pradesh and persuaded my mom to get a doctorate as well, which she eventually did.

My parents were liberal-minded with a progressive outlook. They were never strict with us. And neither were we problem children for them.

My under-graduation was at the same college where dad worked. It was notorious for frequent strikes, and a few that went on for weeks in a row. It offered me ample free time, and I frequently ran off to the nearby SIMA Library at Race Course Road. There, I chanced upon monthly editions of *Capital Market* and *Dalal Street Journal (DSJ)* stock investment magazines. They piqued my attention as I had heard my cousins and two of my uncles regularly chat about stocks whenever we met.

I began to expand my reading selection to *Economic Times, Financial Express, Business India* and other business magazines. I quickly turned into a voracious reader of everything concerning equity stocks, investments, Initial Public Offers

(IPOs), familiarizing myself with various terms – Earnings Per Share (EPS), P/E Multiple, Face Value, Dividend Yield, RONW (Return on Net Worth), Bonus Issue, Market Capitalization, BSE SENSEX, Equity offered at Par or Premium, Proportionate allotment of shares, and gradually became fairly proficient about stock investments for my age.

Over the next years, I had borrowed from my dad more than two lakh rupees in total, in regular installments to invest in both IPOs, and buying small and mid-cap companies' stocks in the secondary market. Unfortunately, I lost much of the money because of my bad investment decisions, from lack of sufficient experience.

However, my dad graciously supported and encouraged me, and never chided me. He was an eternal optimist, and constantly assured me that these stocks I had invested in, would someday recover their prices. He never wanted me to lose the passion.

All the knowledge and the hands-on experience that I gained during those three years of under-graduation generated a strong sense of purpose within me. I wanted to pursue a career in the areas of investment banking and equity research. MBA with a speacialization in Finance was the gateway. I was fortunate to secure a seat at the local university with modest preparation for the entrance test, impressing the interviewers with my knowledge of stocks.

Around the time I completed the final year of MBA, the capital markets were rattled by the Asian Financial crisis that was triggered by the collapse of the Thai Baht. Its fallout had an adverse impact in India too. Many equity research firms were closing shop and it became evident that given the negative circumstances plaguing the economy, I should consider myself lucky to even find a job, forget about a job of my choice.

Thus, I was helplessly glad when I received the offer letter from Standard Chartered Bank within a week of an in-person interview. Even though the job offer was not related to investment banking, I was thrilled. A job at an MNC bank! My parents and sister were ecstatic.

It was the summer of 1997.

I joined as a Credit Analyst, an entry level position in the Credit Underwriting department at Stanchart's Credit Cards Business, India Head-Office in Bangalore.

My job entailed analyzing the credit risk profile of the applicants and making decisions to approve or decline their request for credit. I was allocated the regions of Chennai and Coimbatore, considering I hailed from Coimbatore city.

In a few months, my boss, Lewis Sam was pleased with my work, my energy and the attitude. I was identified as one of the key talents in the team.

The same year, in another part of the country, Aditi too had joined her first job at Pune after completing her MBA from Bangalore. Aditi Narang was an attractive girl. She had an obvious beauty, accompanied with a charming personality, which was amplified by her deeply pleasant voice. Her dad managed a business.

Love could happen anytime, so it is said. With a mere brief touch, the first sight, a smile, a kiss, or a penetrating glance into the eyes. When it happens, it is generally through the likeliest of the ways – with a friend in school or college, a childhood crush, or with a relative within the family, a co-worker or with a total random acquaintance that you meet in the virtual world, or in person.

But my love story was different. In fact, love blossomed between us, only after our last meeting that we were fated to have. It had an abrupt beginning. And it had an abrupt end.

Unfathomable. *Socha bhi na tha.*

1.3

Feeling weary and tired, I got up. The pain and sadness in me vanished, with the residual anger metamorphosing into rage.

It was a rage at her, rage at my dad and mom, rage at myself for letting myself be pushed by her and my parents. At twenty-eight, my life seemed to have ended.

In the past three years, I had on numerous occasions simply wished that I'd vanish into thin air. That would be infinitely better and peaceful than a tortured existence, carrying pain and disgrace in the heart. Until Padma entered my life, I thought I had only one cross to bear which weighed heavily on my soul. But now, I had a second one to deal with.

Clearly, it was Padma now; the other had receded from my brain, for I noticed that the acute anxiety I have been suffering since March 2000 seemed to reduce greatly since I arrived in the US. I wondered if it was the change of place and scene that was helping me to erase the painful memories. Additionally, my mind – which was so fixated on that incident – now had Padma to focus upon.

Staring vacantly at the computer screen, my mind was absorbed in rapid thoughts bursting within.

I can't let my emotions play to her demands. I can't fake it. She cannot force me to love her. She cannot force me to have sex with her. We have been married for just two months and ten days. What is her hurry? Where is her professed patience? All the deep love for me that she constantly preached and claimed, the relentless patience that she put up with my complete indifference to her affections before marriage, why did all that magically disappear immediately after marriage?

How does she think it is her god-given right to have sex with me, just because we are now married? How can she be so uncaring and insensitive to my feelings? Padma had put on a face of a woman of infinite patience to my continued torment of hurtful words that I had hurled at her, post our engagement and until the day of marriage, when I had told her I was not attracted to her physically, and that I did not want to get married to her. And she had been steadfast in being indifferent to what I said, and instead had vowed that she would love me so much, that I simply would have no choice but to love her back.

Strangely, there had been a few occasions, wherein I had found strength in her words, and was taken in by the confidence of her tone. There was a flicker of a hope, that I may be happy with the strong outpouring of her love. But physical beauty was a very big deal for me. A beautiful face, and a beautiful heart – I needed both. I could not settle for just one. One without the other was a huge turn-off.

And since the time we got married, I have seen her other face, and of her frequent and acrimonious outbursts at me. I couldn't bring myself to make love to her yet. My feelings for her have remained the same. The same dislike and aversion, if not greater.

2.3

My office was on Magarath Road, intersecting Residency Road at one end, and near M.G. Road. The office was located inside Raheja Plaza across two floors, adjacent to Shopper's Stop that was housed in the same building.

It felt surreal. The ambience in the building was up-class. The people in the office looked and sounded elite and extremely cultured. I was dazed by everything that I saw, and could not believe how lucky I was to be amidst them.

There were lots of good looking girls and women; that made the place even more interesting.

I had frequent interactions with the customer service teams from Chennai and Coimbatore. They emailed or telexed when they had urgent queries and escalations from the consumers who submitted applications for credit cards. They queried why the apps were still in referral status, what additional documents or information was required for further processing. At times, I was asked why someone was declined and if an exception could be made.

It was easy to get bogged down with the mammoth daily work load, and keep the customer service officer's queries a lower priority. Luckily, I took their queries as equal priority and worked my best to have them resolved, and was pro-active in getting back to them with status updates. Although it was a huge distraction from my regular work, it was simply a part of my job and I fully empathized with the CS officers being blasted by irate customers.

I had completed two months at work, and one afternoon, I received an e-mail of appreciation from Sindhu Shree, Chennai Customer Service Manager on behalf of her entire team who expressed her team's happiness with my speedy resolution of their queries. She marked a copy to Lewis.

15 September 1997

Dear Shyam,

All of us at Customer Support Madras would like to place on record the excellent work and efficient manner in which you handle applications. You really don't give us an opportunity to grumble about turn arounds because everything that is referred to you is resolved very efficiently, and this kind of support is very important for us from the back office. We should probably have an award for back office staff too as otherwise it becomes very difficult to place our appreciation on records.

Thank you once again. Looking forward to your enduring support.

Regards,
Sindhu Shree

Within a minute, Lewis forwarded the mail to his boss, Priyadarshan, copying the entire team, with a note,

Dear Shyam, that I'm proud of you would be an understatement on my part. Please keep up the good work. Cheers, Lewis

Priyadarshan in turn congratulated me, and marked a copy to the Head, Customer Service, Shalini Warrier. She in turned marked a copy to her entire team pan India, showcasing the appreciation, and emphasizing how critical the credit team was to their success, and copied Harpal Duggal - CEO.

15 September 1997

Dear Shyam,

Thanks for the excellent work being done! As you can see, this makes a whale of a difference at the front end, and the entire Customer Service team is very grateful to you for turning around requests in a jiffy. I must indicate here that I get absolutely no escalations from Madras in this regard, unlike what I see at other centers.

Keep up the good work, and the team will keep buying you bouquets!

Regards,
Shalini

The mail went viral and in a matter of an hour, it was forwarded by Harpal Duggal to all his Functional Directs.

It felt great to see congratulatory emails pouring from all of them. I felt grateful to Sindhu Shree and her team for their kind appreciation. She had made me a hero in an instant!

I wrote a thank you note to her, with a copy to Lewis that night before leaving work.

Paresh and Jitu who were of similar age as me, frequently teased me saying that I had wooed all the Chennai Girls, and that I had a big fan club going.

Four months later, when I completed my half-year anniversary, I sent an email to all my colleagues in my department, thanking them for their support.

When I completed nine months on the job, the Sales and Marketing Head wanted to transfer me to their Sales and Marketing analytics team. They checked privately with Lewis who rejected the request.

Although my daily work was very tiring and strenuous, I enjoyed it to the fullest. Each morning, as I entered the two-story building where the office was located, and glanced at the name 'Standard Chartered Bank' screaming in bold Blue and Green on top of the building, a sense of great pride glowed on my face.

One day, I woke up very early in the morning and rode my motorbike to office at 7.30 a.m. Midway, I stopped at a temple and prayed. It was the day of my first anniversary in the company.

I reached my desk, switched on the light in my cubicle and looked around. There was no one else around. I started to frantically type, recalling the lines from my memory. I had gone over this several times the previous night.

I knew that my mail was going to generate shock waves. And when I finished typing, I clicked on the 'Send' button.

1.4

I had been at the browsing center for hours. It was 2:20 p.m. I felt hungry, but I didn't want to go home.

I walked to a nearby Thai restaurant in the same strip mall. Finishing lunch, I drove to Harish's house.

Harish Nair was my colleague and he was one of the very few friends I had, apart from Akash Vermani and Vamsi Parekh in the US. I was new to the country, and been hardly here for six weeks. Harish lived closer to my apartment community. He and his wife, Bindu were evidently surprised to see me when I knocked on their door unannounced.

"Hey Shyam, come on in," he greeted me even as the look of surprise on his face widened when he realized I was alone. "Where is Padma?"

"Padma has not been keeping well. She is resting. I was getting bored, so came over to Walmart. I thought I would just stop by on the way home," I lied and seated myself on the sofa.

"Oh, she is sick! Is it cold or something?"

"Yeah, she is running a slight temperature with a mild sore throat. She has taken some Tylenol," I said.

"Bindu, do you have some *rasam* left from lunch? You can pack it for Padma?"

17

"Ya ya, there is plenty. Shyam, I will pack some for her. Be sure to heat it when you give it to her. It will be good for her throat. Or she can have it with rice."

I nodded.

"So, how is work?" Harish asked.

"Work is good. You know, Harish, I had resolved to never again work in Collections Risk, but here I am, right back in it!"

"Yeah, your H1-B visa processing took much longer than ours. We had ours completed in three months, but yours took close to six months, and the open role in Acquisition Risk that you were to fill in was closed even as Radha Krishnan tried his best to secure your position..."

I had known Radha Krishnan for a few years ever since I had met him at my first job. When I moved from GE Capital International Services (GECIS), Gurgaon to the GE Analytical Center of Excellence (ACOE), Bangalore, Radha who was at ACOE then, left just about the same time and moved to HSBC Auto Finance in San Diego.

Harish, Akash and I were at GE ACOE and we had worked in different teams. They both had worked in Acquisition Risk analytics and I was in Collections Risk analytics.

Akash was the first one to arrive in US, followed by Harish a month later. They worked for Radha Krishnan. When they joined, Radha had confided in them that I was the next one to join their team, as soon as my H1B visa was approved.

"I know," I said, "just two days before I was to fly to the US, Radha Krishnan called me saying he had bad and good news. The bad news was he could not save the role for me this long, and the HR had eliminated the position. But the good news was that there was a position open in a different team in Collections Risk, where I would make a great fit. He had already spoken to Rich Martinez about me. He arranged for a phone interview the next day with Rich and Simon. I was so keen to work under Radha, but bad luck!'

"At least you managed to get to the US and save your job here. After one or two years, I'm sure you can move to our team, Shyam," Harish said.

"That is true! I had already tendered in my resignation at ACOE, and was serving the notice period. And then Radha calls me and asks if I'm okay with joining Collections Risk team," I chuckled as I continued. "What choice did I have!"

I was interrupted by the ringing of the landline phone.

Harish rose from his chair to pick up the cordless.

"Hello. Hey Padma! Shyam is here.... he said you are not keeping well. How are you feeling now?"

I don't know what she said, but she must have picked up on the cue, and managed an answer.

"Okay, one second," said Harish, and he passed the receiver to me.

"Where were you all this time? I was so worried. You didn't tell me where you had gone. I called up Akash first, and then here... I was getting so tensed," she spoke softly.

"I stopped by Harish's place as I had come to Walmart to pick up groceries," I said evenly, with no emotion, looking down on the floor.

"I'm very sorry for what I did. I'm truly sorry. Please come back," she pleaded softly in a sincere tone.

I went silent for a few seconds, and said, "Okay."

I went home with the *rasam* that Bindu had packed. Padma had cooked dinner. I ate and didn't make any conversation, just answering her in monosyllables about her enquiries about Harish and Bindu. And then, I went to sleep.

I woke up early in the morning and left for work, even as she was still sleeping. When I reached my cube, I started to type an email to Padma.

2.4

The e-mail had my resignation letter attached. I had accepted a new job offer at BPL US West Cellular Ltd, in Bangalore, which was a leading provider of cellular services.

I was offered an Assistant Manager role in the Credit Policy Team, directly working for Vishal, with a responsibility of assisting him in the formulation and enforcement of credit policy across the three circles.

Vishal, who was with Stanchart for three years as Credit Analyst, had left two months back to join BPL US West Cellular for a leadership role heading Credit Risk Policy. He had reached out to me.

I had a formal interview with his boss, Mike Dorsam, COO. Vishal had assured me that Mike had liked me and was very impressed, and I should expect an offer letter soon. However, the process had protracted for more than a month. He explained since it was a partnership between BPL and US West, key decisions took time, with Mike Dorsam representing US West had to make sure that the MD, Jayant Kumar representing BPL, was on board with his decision.

Finally, I was given the offer letter the previous day, and it was conditional upon me joining in a week. I was naïve, and didn't know anything better to negotiate on the joining date. The HR lady, Vani Subramaniam bullied me to sign the offer letter at her office when I went to collect it, and I had simply signed on the dotted line. So, I was in a rush to resign at the earliest, and request for being relieved at the soonest possible.

I addressed my resignation to the HR head and marked a copy to Lewis.

28 May 1998

Dear Bala,

It's been great working in Stanchart for a year and I enjoyed being here. Today, 28 May 1998, I complete a year. As I have decided to pursue my career elsewhere, I wish to resign from my services with effect from today and be relieved at the earliest (in a week's time).

I take this opportunity to thank all my colleagues for the help and support they have given me during my association here.

Thanking you.

Yours faithfully,
Shyam

Next, I sent another e-mail to all my co-workers in our team, informing them about my resignation.

It generated shock waves. The Head-office was relatively a small team, and each of us knew one another. Therefore, any resignation aroused general interest, but to quit a company like Stanchart and that too within a year's time had heightened interest, generating curiosity and shock. The news spread and the mails started pouring in from all my colleagues wishing me the best while being sad at my decision to leave.

I used my mind over my heart in making this career move. I felt this was a great career move with a sharp elevation in the job role and higher responsibilities. I couldn't afford to miss this opportunity, especially when I had been approached for the job.

1.5

2 June 2003

To: padma_lakshmi@hotmail.com
Subject: Reply to your "I'm very Sorry"

Yesterday was yet another episode where I felt extremely pained and hurt at your behaviour. This is the fourth time that you have demonstrated this kind of attitude and have employed such words ever since we landed in the US.

Your tone, pitch, body language, attitude in your words – they were so loud, aggressive and uncalled for. It was a repetition of the previous ones. You know something Padma, the one positive thing that I saw in you though I didn't want to get married to you was that I thought you were an innocent and soft-hearted girl.

And when you forced me to get married to you post the engagement, I was just praying to god that perhaps this one positive aspect that I see in you would be an anchor point for the relationship to work out. I saw this as the only silver lining. Sadly, after these four episodes, even that has totally disappeared.

What you did is not so simple that you can wash it away with a 'sorry' and I'm unable to convince myself that your fourth 'sorry' has a value and that you will not repeat it in future.

You know, Padma, life is a whole lot about emotions and feelings. It is not a simple mathematical equation. You can't force me or threaten me or demand from me to give you the kind of emotions you want. It isn't so easy. You didn't understand it before marriage, nor are you able to understand now. Life doesn't work that way. I respect your personal space and would expect likewise from you.

You could take the outside world to look at things in perspective. Diana was wedded to the richest man and the most eligible bachelor in England. But she wasn't happy. It is all about one's feelings, emotions and expectations.

I can't live a life like this for ever. Perhaps someday, you'll understand all this... but then it could be too late for both of us.

Shyam

I hit send and went back to doing my work. I was unable to focus, and could not take my mind off from yesterday's events. I just kept staring at the monitor, replaying all her abusive words in my mind.

You will never find any peace or happiness.
You are such a heartless person.

I was noticing a pattern in yelling and abusing me at the slightest provocation. The first time was when we had moved to US. We were provided a temporary accommodation for two weeks in a hotel. In one of those evenings, we had a tiff and I was mad at her for some reason. I told her I was going to sleep the night on the couch, reading a book. She turned furious and started to scream violently at me, demanding I should sleep with her in the bed.

I was taken aback when I heard her scream for the first time. I had known her only to be a soft and quiet girl in temperament until that moment.

I had reminded her that she was the one who had forced me to get married to her, and asked her what kind of moral right did she have to object at my wish to sleep on the couch.

"So, what if I forced you to get married to me? Why did you allow yourself to get forced by me?" she hollered at me mockingly.

I lost my mind, and flew into a rage when she uttered those words. I had screamed back, "Padma, after having ruined my life, how easy it is for you to say this? I'm indeed a fool, and I kick myself for that now. I should not have given into all your emotional threats of committing suicide if I didn't marry you."

I had continued to rail bitterly with venom, "You have the nerve to ask why I let myself be forced by you. Okay, I will be wiser now. I shall not let myself be forced by you anymore. I will proceed with a divorce."

It was the very first time, I remembered shouting like a mad man in my adult life.

As I was recalling that first incident, and yesterday's along with other instances where she had demanded that I make love to her, I was filled with anger and helplessness at how my life had turned out.

My thoughts were interrupted when Vamsi came over to my cube and asked, "Hey Shyam, what plans do you have today evening?"

2.5

In addition to my sudden resignation, my colleagues found it strange that I had got into the telecom sector, a space that was new and emerging in India. It was 1998, the industry was in its infancy and plenty of uncertainty was associated with its long-term viability.

The cellular operators had obtained licenses to operate in different geographical circles in government auctions with very optimistic expectations of subscriber growth. But the consumer demand was not rapidly growing due to the high call tariffs.

And some of the operators were facing severe cash flow challenges in running day to day operations, making investments in building infrastructure to expand the network footprint to stay competitive, and to attract new subscribers, compounded with the burden of having to pay recurring license fees to the government.

I was ignorant of the big picture ailing the telecom industry, and therefore wasn't perturbed. I had not even consulted my parents about leaving Stanchart, but merely informed them just the day before I resigned.

Within a few months of joining, I realized that this was not the job that I had signed up for. The role lacked any real authority. It was all vested with the three Credit Risk Collections Managers at the individual Circle Offices.

Although on paper, Vishal and I were expected to oversee the three of them, and their teams, we lacked any direct authority over them. They reported to the Commercial Heads at the local circle offices, with a dotted line reporting to Vishal.

My day to day role ended up being a collator of key collections reports from the three circle offices; to consolidate them to send it to Mike Dorsam. The bulk of my work incuded following up with the three managers, and coaxing them to send the reports first thing in the morning every day.

I didn't have any meaningful work, or much work, and thus found my role boring. I commanded some respect, coming from the HQ, but it was not due to my knowledge or expertise. I was raw at twenty-one years, with no great professional experience.

The real action was on the ground, at the Circle offices.

When one of the managers, Nirmal Arora quit, Vishal sent me to Pune for two months to assist them during the transition period until a new person was hired. I was quite excited to go. I would be hands on and would get a better handle on the business by being front and center at the operations site, and could keep myself occupied with purposeful work.

It was my first flight ever. It was a great feeling as the flight took off and dwarfed the city, and soared into the skies, hitting the clouds, and rising above. As it landed at Pune, the city that was until minutes ago, dotted with tiny patches of land, water, houses, roads, vehicles, gradually burst into life-size.

Vishal had assigned me the task of streamlining the acquisition process, look for credit approvals made outside policy guidelines, identify gaps and mitigate, and engage the external vendors and strengthen the quality and timelines of their verification reports. The processes were not very structured compared to what I had seen at Stanchart.

The credit team was on the third floor of the building. I was seated a few cubes away from Maya, who was the credit analyst. She made me feel comfortable and answered my numerous questions patiently as I probed to study and understand their process. I reported regularly to Vishal and to the Commercial Head.

The third floor was constantly bustling with activity; there were people in the accounts department shouting to their co-workers seated nearby about urgent reports to be generated, the commercial head would walk down multiples times in a day to attend meetings, and the external vendors would be talking loudly to the risk executives.

Amidst all the craziness, one day, at lunch time, I noticed a girl from the HR team walking past my cube. She was talking to someone on the phone. Both her face and voice caught my attention. She continued to walk up and down the narrow aisle engrossed in her conversation.

I could not help overhearing her.

"...you know, the reason I walk up and down, while talking, it is that no one gets to hear the entire length of what I am talking."

I found her parading up and down the aisle, merrily chatting on the phone. Did she have no work to do?

She was Aditi Narang.

1.6

Vamsi was born and raised in the US. His parents hailing from Gujarat, had immigrated to the US in the seventies. He was a character. He was fanatical about a few things. He was against gay rights, illegal immigration and a die-hard fan of the Republican Party. He prided himself in being a cowboy and listened only to country music.

He was pretty much out all evenings, drinking at country bars. He was constantly looking for anyone who'd care to hang out with him. He frequently asked Andy, Shoo and me to join him as we all worked in the same team. The first time I accompanied him, I enjoyed a few hours there. Later, to my shock. I found that he was in no mood to consider returning home until the bar closed in the wee hours of the morning.

He had an enormous capacity to drink. I lost count of the number of drinks he had that night; and in his many inspired moments, I found him hurling insinuations at gay people, and at Hispanics who were in the US illegally. And reminding me of the values he stood for, being a proud cowboy, he'd say that he would give his life for his family, friends and his country. In the end, I was grateful that the bar finally closed and we made our way home.

Since that day, I had begun to politely decline his invitations. I came with an excuse saying, "Vamsi, remember I'm married. I can't come out with you all the time."

Drinking like a fish, or being out till the morning hours every day was not my idea of fun.

Yet, he was not discouraged. He continued to ask me every other day. And he never got upset as I turned him down pretty much all the time.

He was a very caring person who had a ready, and easy enthusiasm to explain any query at length. Being brand new to the country, he patiently educated me about many random things related to living in America – the food, etiquettes and pronunciation, especially the Spanish names of the streets in San Diego and Mexican dishes.

I replied, "Don't have any plans."

His face brightened up. "Good! I'm going to the night club … do you want to come along?"

"Yes," I said swiftly.

He was visibly surprised at my unusual readiness.

I was feeling sore in my heart, and didn't want to go home and see Padma's face, if I could help it.

"Let's leave work at sixish. We will drive to my apartment. Have a few drinks at my place and then head to the night club."

"Okay. You know, I have never been to a night club before…"

"Yeah, don't worry. You'll be fine."

I didn't bother to inform Padma that I'd be home late. She would obviously be concerned, but what did I care!

At his apartment, we sat on the couch as he poured me a drink.

"Shyam, here is the deal. There is no cover charge in this club, the entry is free, but you are expected to order drinks when you get in there. That's how they make money. And you tip them a dollar for each drink. That is the etiquette.

"The women on the stage will be topless. They perform for each song. When they are finished, they will crawl to the edge of the stage. If you are seated in the front row, you are obliged to tip them. You can tuck in a dollar into their panty string, or hand it to them. You cannot touch them though. You are not allowed to, and it is illegal in California and I think in most other states..."

"But how will I insert a dollar bill into their panty string without touching them?"

"Light brushing is fine. But watch out for the cue. If you see everyone placing the dollar bill on the floor of the stage, then that is what you do too.

"But here is the deal. There will be women on the floor as well, who will walk up to you and ask if you want a lap dance. Each may cost fifteen to twenty dollars for one song, depending on the girl. They set their own price. They should tell you beforehand, but if they don't, you ask for it. You cannot touch them when they are performing. It is against law. And if you do, they will remind you not to touch them. If you still do, there are bouncers everywhere around in the club monitoring, who will give you a warning and eventually ask you to leave.

"Another thing, if you end up conversing with a dancer off stage, the etiquette is to give her money for the interaction; roughly a dollar a minute. If you don't want to talk to someone, be direct but polite about it, so as not to waste her time."

I nodded my head, absorbing everything that he said, wondering what the night club was going to look like.

We drove to the club. Cheethas was just few miles away from Vamsi's house.

We found some empty seats in the front row, which was very close to the stage. Vamsi ordered the drinks. The bartenders were pretty, every one of them. The music was in full blast. A tall blonde with barren legs walked to the stage on heels, with just a bra and a short skirt. She held both her hands to the pole and drifted her body away from it, swaying gently. The drinks arrived.

She unbuttoned her bra, and was completely topless. For the next few minutes, she danced around the pole, climbing on to it, and sliding down. Next, she removed the skirt, all naked with just a panty. I finished my drink, and asked for another from the pretty bartender flashing a bright smile.

The dancer finished her performance, and everyone was cheering. She started at one end of the semicircular stage, on her knees and crawled across with her bum facing the audience, head tilted back, wearing a wide fake smile; and occasionally tapping her bum with her hand to please the audience, as she moved to the other end. Vamsi stood up, pulled out his wallet and took two-dollar bills. Folded them length wise, and as the girl approached us, he made eye contact with her, dabbed his head and slid the dollar bills between her bum and the thong string. I mimicked Vamsi and slid two-dollar bills.

I ordered another drink. Vamsi was amused. It was the third drink I was having in quick succession.

"Shyam, having fun?"

"Yeahh," I said.

"Do you want a lap dance?"

"Okay ya, where can I get one?" I asked.

"Right there," he pointed to seats far away from the stage, in the middle and far corners of the floor. "The girls will come and ask you when you are seated in that area. Each girl has her price, but it would be either $15 or $20 for a song. Find that out before you go ahead."

I nodded. I felt light. Felt happy. My lingering worries of Padma vanished from my mind. This felt like a nice place to be in. When I had walked in through the door, catching a quick glimpse of the pretty girls, I felt a surge of sharp pain pierce through my heart. I was sad that I was not married to someone as attractive as them. Now, even that painful feeling had dimmed with the drinks.

I ordered a fourth drink. I knew I was a no match for Vamsi. He had gulped more drinks than I cared to count. Two girls came and asked me if I would like a lap dance. I smiled politely, and said, "Thank youuu, but laterrrrr."

I didn't find them attractive enough.

My speech became slow as I asked Vamsi if we could come again the next day.

"Yeahhhh, I come here all the time. I told youuuuu, you would love it."

"I'm saddd, I'm veryyyy saddd. I'm not happy with my wife. I want to come here again tomorrow," I blurted out.

"Whyy? What is the deal, Shyamm?" he asked in a drawl.

"She forced me to get married to her. I do not like her. She yells and screams. Will youuuuu help me, Vamsiii?" I was slurring.

He instinctively grabbed my shoulder, "Shyam, I'm a cowboy. You know what cowboys doo? They take care of their countryy, familyy and friendss," he blurted out.

"I'm sooooo frightened, Vamsi. Her brother-in-law told me he will make my life miserable. This is not Indiaaa. It is the US where the legal system is veryyyyy strict. All it takes is just a phone call... those were his words."

Even in the drunken state, Vamsi's temper rose, and he thundered, "Why doesn't sheee leave you alone? Why does she harrasss youuu? What does she think, you have no one? Let me tell you thiss. Shyammm, you are not just my buddyyyyy. You are my familyyyy. I will stand by you, no matter what. That is what cowboys doooo."

I was touched by his words. A wave of gratitude swirled in for him.

"Hi, would you like a lap dance?" a girl cooed into my ears.

I turned my face to look at her, and nodded a yes swiftly. She was very attractive.

"Come, follow me," she said and guided me to a seat in the far corner.

"I'm Emily. It is $20 a song. How many songs would you like?" she asked.

"Maybeee twooo songs, I said."

She flashed a smile. She stripped every piece of her clothes, excepting the panty. She rested her hands on the chair across at both ends of my head, twirled her body seductively, moved her hips, and danced around me. She raised her hand to pull her hair up, teasingly came closer to my face and in one swaying motion, let the hair down. They fell on my face for a few fleeting seconds before she pulled them back and moved away from me. She was teasing me, along with her gyrations. I was enjoying myself immensely.

She smiled, "Do you want another dance?"

Before I knew, she said I owed her $180. I didn't think I asked for nine dances with her and told her so. She retorted that I had indeed did. By then, Vamsi came to my side as he saw us engaged in an argument.

Vamsi challenged her, taking my word. She called the bouncer. The bouncer was rude, and said I owed $180, and there was nothing to argue, else he would call the cops. I paid off the money and we left.

I reached home, somehow; I don't know how. I remember speeding and taking sharp turns. Vamsi had stayed back in the car in the parking lot and had driven home in the morning when he turned sober.

We had no cellphones. Padma was expectedly extremely anxious, not knowing my whereabouts. She was relieved to see me when I knocked on the door. It was past eleven.

"Where were you? Do you know how panic stricken I was?"

"I had gone out with Vamsiiiii," I said as I kicked off my shoes and removed the socks.

I went to the bedroom. She followed me.

"Why were you so late?" she asked with fear writ on her face.

I lay down on the bed, covered myself with a quilt, and started to mumble.

"I droove verrry fassstt. I did noooot wantt to liveeee. I wanted to crasssh and diee."

I kept muttering incoherently before I dozed off to sleep.

2.6

I had found the people and the work culture at the BPL Bangalore office similar to Stanchart. The leadership team was down to earth, friendly and warm. But Pune office was very different.

It reeked of a house of people with bloated egos – each busy promoting their own interests and agenda in a slugfest with other teams. The business operations had no strong systems and processes in place, and we were always in constant fire-fighting mode, dealing with one issue or the other.

Some of the senior leaders in the organization did not take kindly when I addressed them by first name, as was the practice in Stanchart or in the BPL head-office. They wanted to be addressed with a 'sir' as a suffix.

This added to my existing woes of being unhappy with my role.

Around that time, Global Trust Bank was on a hiring spree across the nation. The bank was expanding its branch network aggressively, and had put out newspaper ads calling for qualified people to apply for various banking positions.

I decided to apply for a job there. I did not have a copy of my resume with me. I called up Radhika, and told her there were few hard copies of my resume in my room in Coimbatore, and asked her to courier it to me at my Pune office address.

It was a week and I had not received them yet.

One evening, Aditi walked up to me.

She caught my glance, and yelled out to me aloud with a befuddled look, "Are you Shyam V.E.N.K.A.T?" before shifting her eyes on to the paper again.

I was amused that my last name was being hollered. I nodded my head. Coming closer to me, she said, "If you are looking for a job, you should be careful enough not to send the resume to the company that you work for."

I was disarrayed. I asked, "What are you saying? I don't understand." And no sooner did I say that, realization set in. I thought to myself, oh shit, Radhika's packet had somehow landed up in the HR's desk!

I panicked, but gathered my nerves and said, "My friend wanted to model his resume on mine. I had asked my sister to send it. But how did it reach HR? Can I have it back, please?"

"Okay, but Boss asked me to give this back to him. You could collect it from him."

That was my very first interaction with Aditi.

I got worried. Her boss, Mukund Desai, was not a nice man. He could make things difficult for me if he escalated this to Corporate HR. My heart beat fast. Flushed with anger, I walked to Mukund's office later in the evening, and said casually, "Hi Mukund, can I have my papers?"

"What papers?" he smirked.

"It's not fair. Can I have them back, please?"

"I don't have it, and I am not telling your boss."

I stared at Mukund, and walked away from his door. I was not worried about Vishal, knowing he too wasn't happy in BPL. My concern was the corporate HR getting wind of this.

The next morning, I went to Aditi and complained to her, "He is so unprofessional, Aditi. He is refusing to give my resume back to me."

"I know, he is," she said. "Don't worry, Shyam. I will talk to him and get it for you."

1.7

When I woke up in the morning, the previous night's incident at the night club returned to my memory. I tried to recall how I had got back home. Did Vamsi drop me back? No, I had driven home myself. I was so drunk, I wondered how I managed to reach safely.

And I recalled what I had jabbered to Padma before I went to sleep. I didn't know why I said all that.

I pulled myself out of the bed, brushed my teeth, and took a shower. Padma was already up. She was unusually quiet. She offered me breakfast and I ate. She packed a lunch. I left for work.

When I returned home in the evening, Padma asked me, "Shyam, I want to talk to you. Can we step out for a walk?"

"What is it?" I asked her, mechanically showing no interest.

"I have to tell you something."

"Okay, maybe later. I have just come from work, and I'm having a splitting headache," I lied.

"Shyam, this is very important. You are going to be happy to hear it."

I had no hint of what she meant by that. But it was enough to pique my interest.

"Okay, let's go."

We stepped out of the apartment, climbed down the stairs and began to walk around the apartment community.

She was silent for several minutes, and we kept walking. I was eager to know what she wanted to say that could make me happy. There was only one thing I deeply wished for. I wanted her to disappear from my life. But that was wishful thinking.

I pretended to be uninterested, waiting for her to break the silence and start speaking.

"I have been giving this a serious thought..." she spoke finally. "There has been lot of tension between us both lately. We both need some space from each other, to cool it off. I have decided to go to New Jersey to my sister's house *and...*" she said with an emphasis on 'and'.

She looked up at my face and continued, "...and I will not come back until you call me back."

What I heard was unfathomable. I wanted to give her a hundred hugs.

I wondered what triggered her sudden decision, but I didn't ask her. I suspected it was probably driven by the previous night's episode. I had told her in my drunken stupor how I was speeding, wanting to end my life. And maybe she spoke to her sister about this. And her sister must have panicked. What if Padma had been in the car with me then? Or what if I was driven to do something like that in future with Padma in the car.

I merely asked, casually, "When do you intend to go to your sister's house?"

"Tomorrow," she said.

I was floundered. I asked her in a rare kind tone, "Padma, are you serious?"

"Yes, I have packed my bags. Anita has booked me for a morning flight tomorrow. Can you drop me to the airport before you leave for work?" she asked.

"Of course, I will," I said feeling grateful.

"Anita has informed my parents about everything. My parents were shocked to hear this. They didn't know of anything that was going between us. I will not come back until you call me back. I hope when I'm away, you will realize how much I love you," she said.

I said nothing.

I was happy that she was leaving, and happier that she emphasized she would not come back unless I called her. But why would I call her back? No way.

I knew our marriage would not last for too long; but never did I expect it would end this soon, and in such a smooth, civil manner.

I felt a deep sense of gratitude to Vamsi and muttered a silent thanks to him. Had I not gone out with him to the night club, and returned home jabbering, Padma would not have left.

The next morning, I dropped Padma off at the airport.

I had a rush of euphoria as I saw her off. My heart felt light after a very long time and felt assured about the prospect of permanent freedom from her, which until now seemed to be a distant possibility.

2.7

Life was comfortable in the company guest house. Breakfast and dinner was prepared by the caretaker, and it was a sheer luxury to not having to fend for myself here, unlike in Bangalore. I got a handsome daily stipend that I could spend lavishly for lunch, and still save money.

At Pune, I was doing something truly useful, and adding value, and keeping myself engaged and busy. The days rolled fast.

A month and a week later, one day I walked up to Aditi. I was dressed in my favourite bright blue Allen Solly shirt and pale grey Allen Solly trousers.

"Hi Aditi."

"Hi Shyam! You are all dressed up."

I smiled and said, "Well, I am a little sad these days!"

"Why is that?"

"That I have to return to the Bangalore office in a week."

"Oh! Is it because of someone in your team that you don't want to leave?" she asked cheekily.

I understood that she was hinting at Maya with whom I had been working extensively ever since I came to the Pune office.

"Nooo!" I protested, "I'm sad because I have taken a liking for this place and I'm quite enjoying what I am doing here."

"Has it been two months since you came here?"

"Yes, it's been a month-and-a-half."

"It seems like yesterday."

"I know," I said.

I then asked, "Aditi, I need your help to co-ordinate to book my return flight tickets to Bangalore, for next week. Can you do this for me?"

"Sure, but you have to give me a treat for helping you."

I looked at her, and smiled. As I was about to make a reply, we were interrupted by Maya.

"Oh, there you are. I have been looking for you all over!"

"What is it Maya?" I asked.

She drew me aside and asked in a suspicious tone, "What's up? You are all dressed up today, Shyam." She then continued with her questions seeking clarification on a credit policy document.

Later in the evening, I called Aditi on her cell. I had her number from the office contact list that contained the cell phone and office landline numbers of key contacts. It was pinned in most cubicles, and I had one too. I had seen Aditi leave the office a little early.

"Hello"

"Hi Aditi! It's me, Shyam"

She said a short, 'hi'. I was sure she was startled to receive a call from me.

"So, tell me, where do you want to go for the treat?"

She replied after a few seconds, "I was just kidding, Shyam. Thanks. I have reached home."

I quickly said, "Aditi, I was kidding of course. Why'd I waste my money on you?"

After a brief silence, she said, "You are very smart."

"I will see you tomorrow," I said smiling.

After I returned to Bangalore, Aditi and I kept in occasional touch over emails. We had become good friends.

1.8

I shared Padma's departure with Vamsi when I reached office. He was happy for me, but didn't ask for any further details.

I was savoring my new-found freedom in my mind and spirit, and a week passed. Padma called me one evening, and for the very first time, since she had entered my life, I was happy to talk to her. After all, she had been such a sweetheart to leave me. I'd be a very good friend, I promised to myself.

After the pleasantries, she asked me when I was going to call her back. She repeated that she would not come back to live with me until I asked her to return. As I heard her words, my heart sank. I was crestfallen. She was still harboring a hopeless hope, contrary to my expectations. From then on, I stopped taking her calls. And when she left me voice messages, I never called her back.

Expectedly, this made her furious. She made several calls every day at different times in the morning and evenings, and on weekends. And her sister, and brother-in-law Adarsh too tried reaching me, occasionally leaving messages asking me to call them back.

I was certain I could not live with her, nor wanted to. So I continued to avoid her calls and everyone else's.

But I wasn't sure if I could simply refuse to take her calls, from a legal standpoint in this country, as she was my wife.

Adarsh's words were constantly poking at the back of my mind. In one of her angry outbursts when she was here, she had called her sister in front of me, and started to simply cry without uttering a word. Her sister panicked, imagining something grave had happened, and gave the phone to her husband. Adarsh had asked Padma to pass the phone to me. When I had answered it, he had asked me politely but firmly, "Shyam, what is going on?"

I had told him, "Adarsh, she is constantly fighting with me. I can't live with her. I'm not physically or mentally attracted to her."

He cut me short in mid-sentence and said, "Let's go legal on the separation. I have just one sister-in-law and I will use everything in my power to make your life miserable. This is not India. It is the US, where the legal system is very stringent. Okay, sir?"

I had frozen at his words with shock and fear.

I was thus paranoid. And was careful not to do anything stupid.

Not wanting to take any chances, I called 911. The lady asked me if it was an emergency. I said no, and briefly explained my situation. She said an officer would call me back in a couple of days. I thanked her.

The next day evening, my home phone rang.

"Can I speak to Shyam Venkkaat?" a lady's voice asked.

"Yes, this is him."

"I'm Officer Kathy Ferguson. I'm calling from the San Diego Mission Valley Police department. We received your note yesterday, so how can I help you?"

"Ma'am, thanks for calling back. I'm in a little situation. I got married in India a few months ago. I didn't want to get married to this girl, but I was forced to, against my wishes..."

"Oh boy!"

"We got separated three weeks ago and she has gone to live with her sister in New Jersey. Since then, the girl and the girl's sister and her brother-in-law are calling me repeatedly. I feel harassed. I don't want to talk to them. I have not been taking their calls, or returning their messages."

"Are they threatening you?"

"Not yet. But, I wanted to know, if I have the right *not* to take their calls. Or am I legally obligated to respond, although we are living separately, we're still technically married?"

"No, you are fine. If they threaten you with harm or any physical violence, then you can seek a restraining order. She or her family member will not be allowed to come anywhere within a certain number of miles close to where you live."

"Thank you officer, I'm so relieved to hear this."

"Is there anything else I can help you with?"

"That was all, officer, I really appreciate your time, thank you."

"Okay, have a good evening. I'm sorry to hear about your situation. But don't worry. Take care and if you ever receive a threat, don't hesitate to call us, my dear," she said with an affectionate chuckle.

I heaved a sigh of relief.

2.8

BPL US West was experiencing cash flow challenges, like most other telecom operators. Eight months had passed since I had joined. It started to re-structure its operations to cut down costs, and one of its focus, as part of the larger exercise, was in reducing the number of leadership positions in the head-office, and moving them to the circle offices, where they were needed the most.

Vishal was sent to Pune to head the Collections Operations. He was not happy at all, but he had no choice. Less than a month later, I was informed by the HR Leader that my services were required in the Kerala Circle. Akshay Nair, who was the credit risk collection manager, had taken a leave of long absence due to health issues, and I was asked to join the Cochin office as early as the following Monday to help Kishore, who was holding the fort in Akshay's absence. I was told Kishore and I would be working in Collections Operations directly under Karun Menon, Commercial Head, until Akshay returned.

I wasn't happy about the move either. Bangalore was a glamorous place to be in. I didn't want to go to Cochin. And, it would be disastrous for my future career moves. But I had no choice as well. I wrote to Aditi, informing her about my transfer.

13 February 1999

From: Shyam@bplblr.com
To: Aditinarang@bplpune.com

Hi Aditi,
I am moving to the Cochin Office on Monday (on a transfer.) Do keep in touch. Will send you my mobile number and email address.

Take care,
Shyam

My flight was at 11.00 a.m. on Monday. I felt miserable, and apprehensive. I had a light breakfast and headed to the nearby temple. I prayed and sat there silently for thirty minutes and then took an auto to the airport.

Three hours later, I was in Cochin. Similar to the Pune office, the Cochin office was a heavy contrast to the look and feel of the head office. There was chaos and confusion everywhere. People were conversing as much in Malayalam as in English. I was given a cold welcome by Karun Menon. He opined that I had only worked in the HQ, and would have no understanding or knowledge of business operations at the ground. He sounded very skeptical of the value-add I was to bring to the table, in the role.

But Cochin had its charm. I was to meet Annie there.

1.9

My dad called me.
"Hi Daddy!"

"Shyam, how are you doing? How is work?"

"It's good. Simon and Rich, both seem to be happy with my work. The auto business is new, but I'm learning. Work is very hectic," I lied.

It was easy work, but I lied to be consistent with what I had told Padma on many occasions about the reason for me coming late from work.

Padma called my dad directly. She often called him to seek guidance on how to deal with me, and for her own mental strength. Dad was an eternal optimist. He kept reassuring her everything was going to be fine.

"Okay, good. You need to work hard to make an impression. But it is also important to keep a balance between work and family."

I was surprised. Does he not know yet that Padma has left? I had not told anyone, but I suspected that Padma must have called him by now and told him everything.

"Yes Daddy," I said and asked, "How are you?"

"I'm doing great. I'm just worried about you. You are a very nice person. All the things you are doing to Padma, I have told her that is not your true character. I have asked her to be supportive. It is a big change for you.

"She loves you very much. Call her back. You are both behaving like kids. You should live happily. You will understand in due course, fights are part of marriages."

"Daddy, you don't know how she yells and screams at me. She was so quiet before marriage, and now she is very combative."

"I know everything, *Kutti*. The other day when she shouted at you before she left for New Jersey, it was only because of me. I was the one who advised her to get aggressive with you to make you understand. It's not her. That has backfired. Anyway, that's okay. She is an innocent child. Her father and mother also spoke to me yesterday. I have assured them not to worry.

"I have told them Shyam does not do things like this. He has otherwise been a good boy. He will call Padma back to San Diego. Okay?"

"Okay Daddy..." I said meekly. I never talked back or protested loudly with him.

And even when I protested, it was not effective. Dad simply repeated his message gently, many number of times in my calls with him, without heeding to my grievances.

I started avoiding dad's calls too. I only kept in touch with my mom whom I called during her day when I was certain that dad had gone to college. Or I disconnected the call when dad answered the phone.

Some of my cousins and uncles started to counsel me, asking me to call Padma back and I stopped taking their calls too. A few persisted via e-mails. I turned myself into an island, cutting off my interaction with my family members.

Amidst this, Paresh called me from Delhi.

"How are you doing, dude? I called your home and your mother gave me your number. When I enquired about how your married life was going, she started to cry, and asked me to speak to you. Shyam, is everything okay? What is going on?" he asked worriedly.

Paresh and I were quite close. We had kept in touch since the Stanchart days. He got married a year ago, and was working for American Express in Gurgaon now.

I came clean and told him everything, bracing myself for a lecture on my actions. Surprisingly, he didn't say anything.

When I finished, Paresh said in a grave tone, "Shyam, to be honest, when your mother began to cry, I knew all was not okay with your marriage. You won't believe me when I say this, what are the odds of a similar thing happening to me as well, almost like one in a million, right?"

"What are you saying, Paresh?" I cried with dismay.

"Shyam, exactly, this is blowing my mind. You are going through exactly what is happening in my life. Just that, in my case, things have gotten very, very ugly. We had issues after marriage. One day, when I returned home from work, I found she had taken all her jewellery and simply disappeared. When I called her, she said she had gone back to her parent's house, and she could not live with me. I tried to persuade her to come back, and she refused to."

"You were happy to be marrying her, I know," I said. "I recall the excitement in your voice when I called to wish you on the day of your wedding. But was she forced into a marriage

by her parents? Why else would she walk out within a year?"
I asked.

He didn't reply, but continued, "I kept trying to call her back for four months, hoping she would change her mind. Neither she, nor her parents would talk to me. Exasperated, I said, if she wasn't coming back and did not want to live with me, I'd file for a divorce. Her father said her daughter would not agree to that either."

"God, I can't believe this, Paresh. You are going through the same thing," I said.

"And this is nothing, Shyam. Wait, till I tell you all the things the girl's parents have done, you will be shocked."

He continued, "After I told her dad that I'd file for divorce, he sent a letter to my HR director detailing the marital issue, and asking that I be dismissed from work. He even called and spoke to my HR director on the phone. Can you believe it? I'm shocked how he even managed to get my director's name."

I froze. Adarsh's words echoed in my mind.

"What happened then? How did you get to know of all this?" I asked rapidly, my heart beating fast.

Paresh's voice cracked, as he spoke with emotion, "It is the grace of god, Shyam. I got lucky that the HR director, whom her father had spoken to, is a divorcee. He called me to his office and said they had received a letter of complaint against me from my wife; they want you fired. 'Obviously, we are not going to do anything like that. This is strictly your personal matter. I have said that to your father-in-law. The company won't interfere. But I felt it was important I made you aware of this. I have been a victim of this myself and I'm very empathetic. You are a high performer, and I don't want this to hurt you or your work. Not just that, this is purely a personal matter'. Those were his exact words."

I felt dizzy, as I heard this.

Could such a thing happen to me? Luckily, I'm working in the USA; and don't think Padma or her family will do anything like that, or even if they did reach out to my HR, it shall have no consequence.

I asked grimly, "Did they stop with that?"

"No!"

"Oh," I said anxiously.

"Her dad and brother kept calling me to Kolkata. They said I should come over and speak to them and their family elders and then only will they decide the next course of action. If the elders agreed, she would sign the divorce papers and give consent.

"Knowing what they had done behind my back, I had lost my trust, and didn't feel comfortable about going and meeting them. But her dad kept persisting for about a month. The more he persisted, the more, I smelled trouble, and refused giving some excuse or the other. And then the worst thing in my life happened..."

He made a pause, as his voice choked again, "Cops came to my dad's house one morning and arrested my parents."

"What! Why did that happen?" I asked in alarm.

"My wife had filed a complaint at the local police station that my parents and I had harassed her for dowry after marriage. This is the thing, Shyam. You will be shocked to hear that the Anti-dowry law or Section 498-A is a draconian law. It is skewed so much in favour of women. All it takes is for them to merely make a written complaint alleging dowry harassment. And that provides the cops the power to arrest any immediate family members of the guy, and put them behind bars. And this law does not require her to provide any evidence. It is treated as a non-bailable offence.

"I'm sharing all this with you, so that you don't go through what I have gone through. Even if the complaint is false, you shall be presumed guilty until you prove that you are innocent. So, you must be careful, Shyam. I wouldn't want this to happen to you."

I freaked. Beads of sweat broke out on my face.

My situation had become more complex with dire consequences. My anxiety transformed into a rage for several minutes, as my mind seethed with fury at my dad, and at everyone who had forced me into this marriage.

I was held accountable to that word 'yes', merely because it was uttered from my lips. All that counted was a legal evaluation of whether I had uttered a yes or not. Some of my cousins and uncles too, when they counselled me, employed the same logic and view-point, that this is a one-way road to marriage. The engagement had taken place, and there was just no exit option.

No one acknowledged the core issue, or ventured into having a real conversation with me. I was just not attracted to her. That was the issue. As simple as that. Yes, I'm not physically attracted to her. No, I'm not claiming I'm a handsome guy, so why am I being countered with 'Have you looked at yourself in the mirror?' every time I spell out the reason. What do I do, when I don't feel the attraction, when I don't feel the chemistry?

Yes, I might come across as being completely shallow but things like marriage should start with the best foot forward. I wanted both a beautiful face and a beautiful heart. One without the other was a big turn-off. This wish was defined by my life experiences, and all the beautiful and wonderful women I had regularly met since I was in my teens.

But everyone simply counselled me about the virtuous path to follow, which was to marry the girl, and assuring me that everything would just fall into place after marriage.

Padma was not the first girl I had met. There were many before.

I was going through a severe bout of depression, thanks to my work situation, affecting my confidence and sense of self-worth. To add to it, girls I met and greatly liked, reciprocated with complete disinterest, while dad continued to pressurize me to marry the next girl whose marriage proposal came his way.

Right from the first girl, my dad had been insistent I say yes. The more I refused saying that they weren't good looking, the more determined he had become in convincing me.

It was very frustrating. I wanted to get married. But most of the women I met through the formal marriage proposals weren't pretty. And the more of these women I met, I got demoralized and uncertain about the possibilities of finding someone I liked through this formal match-making process.

Finally, I succumbed to the cumulative weight of the pressure, burdened with a weak mind and spirit. In one weak moment, I said 'yes' to Padma, only to regret within a day and change my decision. But it was too late, I was told, for the engagement date was finalized that very same day, and the engagement hall was booked. I was screamed at and was asked whether I was out of my mind to even consider such a preposterous thing of cancelling the engagement. It was a serious matter of prestige and honour. It would be a loss of face, what would you tell them? How can you even play with the girl's emotions, someone who is elated to know that you have agreed to marry her?

I had dreamt all along, that I would marry the girl of my dreams; my life lay in shambles now. How could this happen to me?

Unfathomable. *Socha bhi na tha.*

The fear returned and superseded the emotions of anger and rage.

I called my sister and told her what had happened with Paresh and said we needed to be careful. If Padma's family did anything at all, my parents and Radhika would be the easy targets.

Radhika listened to me, and when I completed, she laughed saying I was getting freaked out unnecessarily. She said that Padma's parents would never do such a thing. I didn't debate with her, for I was relieved to see her being dismissive of my fears.

2.9

"Can I speak to Priya?"

A pause and Priya's name is yelled into the speaker by the attendant. Moments later, a thin feeble voice was heard.

"Hello?"

"I wanted to speak to Priya."

"Yes, that's me."

"I'm sorry. I know you are not her."

"What? I am not whom?"

"You are not Priya, I know."

"What! So, you think you can see through the phone?"

"I don't have to. You don't sound like Priya."

"What do you mean? This is my voice." (giggles)

I'm being teased, I told myself.

"I meant, that she has a sweet voice and your voice is far from it."

"I am flattered."

I chose not to respond and said, "Really nice talking to you, but can I speak to Priya?"

She laughed out loudly, "And who do you think you were speaking to all this while!"

Before I could answer, I heard her shout to someone distant amidst her giggles, "Hey, I think this call is for you. Your friend must be mad with me!"

"Hello"

"God, Priya, there you are! Who was that?"

"Shyam, that's my friend Annie Priya. This mix up happens occasionally."

Priya Nair had been my next-door neighbour at Coimbatore where they rented a house for a few years when I was in the twelfth grade. I bumped into her randomly on a visit to Music World Shop at MG Road. She was in a rush and gave me her hostel number, asking me to call her later.

And this was my first interaction with Annie Priya. Thereafter whenever I called Priya Nair, I got to chat with Annie. We had become friends and Priya Nair didn't seem to mind at all.

We had few more conversations over the phone in the next few weeks. One Saturday, she called me on my cellphone and asked if I wished to meet her. I agreed, for I too was curious to see the girl who giggled wildly over the phone.

I went to her hostel, and told the office staff that I had come to meet Annie. They made an announcement on the speaker, and asked me to wait. I waited outside, leaning against my bike parked under a tree.

After about five minutes, I saw a girl walking towards me, smiling and giggling, alternately.

As she came closer to me, she asked, "Shyam?" And held out her hand.

I said, "Hi Annie."

My curiosity had turned into a plain disinterest when I saw her. She looked so ordinary.

She said, "I want you to know, there are three rules to our friendship. One, you should never call me at my office until I say so; two, we can only be friends; three, you should know that I am already engaged to someone."

I was numb with shock for a moment. It sounded strange and funny, because she had wanted to meet me that day. It was a mere first meeting.

All the charm that I had seen radiating out of her conversations seemed glaringly absent with respect to her looks. And to compound my disinterest, I was irritated by the way she conducted herself.

Every day since then, she called me to wish a 'good morning' and talked to me precisely for less than half a minute, and each time with unfailingly regularity, she ended the call abruptly.

I could never understand as to why she wanted to make such a short call every day. Those brief conversations continued for several weeks.

And gradually the friendship between us grew.

1.10

Padma called me again and this time I picked her call. This was the second call I ended up answering ever since she had left.

"Hello," I said.

"How are you, Shyam?"

"I'm okay, Padma," I said slowly. "Work in the office has been very hectic. And on top of it, I'm having to manage the house."

"You never called me even once after I left for New Jersey?"

I remained quiet.

"You have not been answering my calls at all. I have been trying to reach you, and you just ignore it all," she raised her voice.

I didn't say a word.

"I told you I'm not coming back unless you call me. You must decide fast. You cannot take forever to decide. Or send all my stuff back!" she screamed.

My heart raced. "Okay," I said. I was scared to say anything more.

"And my mother wants to talk to you. She is coming to the US to see me, but she wants to talk to you before leaving India. Please call her."

I said nothing.

She hung up.

I called up Radhika and told her I couldn't talk to Padma's mother. What would I tell her? Padma's parents had every right to be mad at me. I felt awful that I was causing pain to so many people.

The next instant, I flared with anger, lamenting how dad had forced me into this marriage, and destroying both mine and Padma's lives. Radhika said, "*Re*, you know what Dad says. He says he never forced you. It was your decision, and only when you said 'yes', he proceeded forward."

I snapped back, acidly, "*Akka*, why is he translating it in a literal sense? What do I do? He was relentlessly persuading me into agreeing to marry Padma; and in one weak moment I said yes, only to retract the next day."

Radhika said, "*Thamba*, if only you were so strong then, as you are now, this situation would have been avoided *ra*. Don't worry. Focus on your work and exercise daily. You know when you work-out, endorphins are released. They are the happy hormones. Stay happy *ra*. Let's see how we manage this, but be happy."

2.10

It took me almost two months for the new work email account to be set up at the Cochin office. When I got transferred to Cochin, the Bangalore IT team told me that their counterparts in Cochin office will be setting a new email account for me in their server, and my email address will switch from shyam@bplblr.com to shyam@bplkoc.com and until then, I had no access to my email box. I didn't know why it took them that long.

I wasn't happy at all about my work. I didn't see a long-term future in my role. Karun mentioned he would determine a permanent role for me after a few months; as he was racking his brains to think where I'd make the best fit.

Meanwhile, I was temporarily assigned to travel across Kerala with Kishore on a collections drive to meet big ticket customers who had defaulted on their payments and ran high outstanding balances. We had to resolve billing disputes if any and collect money from them.

I travelled to many towns across Trivandrum, Kottayam, Kollam, Trichur, Chenganacherri. Apart from Cochin, most of the offices in the other towns were smaller centers and with fewer people; it was easier to bond with almost everyone. However, I did not like the core nature of work. It was unsystematic and rather crude.

Around mid-April, the IT team informed me that my account was set up. When I logged in for the first time, I was very thrilled to see Aditi's email pop up where she had replied promptly to the e-mail that I had written before leaving Bangalore.

15 February 1999

Hi,

It was very nice to see your email. How are you doing?

All the very best. Enjoy whatever comes to you and don't worry.

Keep in touch.

Rest fine,

Aditi

I instantly wrote back to her.

12 April 1999

Dear Aditi,

Ditto here. It was a great feeling and more so to see your mail when I accessed my new mail id for the first time. (It just got set up, and I could see your e-mail today.)

You had rightly suggested that it's better to enjoy what one is doing rather than worry about it. I am learning to do that.

*Did I hear that you want to move to the Bangalore office?
What did you do on April 1st?*

Do reply.

Bye,
Shyam

And we traded a few e-mails over the next few days. Felt good
to be connected to an old friend, especially when I was yet to
make any new friends at the Cochin office.

14 April 1999

*No, I am not keen about moving to Bangalore coz my folks are
in Delhi. I had wanted to go there, but there is no spot free as of
now. So, I am here. And enjoying, or rather, managing.*

*The 1st of April was fun. Played a prank on someone. Made
someone believe it is the boss's birthday. Told him to arrange
a party and stuff!! What else do you expect from a notorious
person like me?*

*Rest is all the same. Good to know that you have settled
down and enjoying life. All the best.*

Rest fine.

Bye,
Aditi

16 April 1999

*If you ask me, you were pretty decent on April 1st. I couldn't
think of anything good, so just called up few friends and told
them that I was head over heels in love with them. Blah! Blah!
While one dismissed it as a poor joke, others were really wild*

(read disappointment!) when reminded them in the end it was the 1ˢᵗ of April.

Bye,
Shyam

Whenever I met with Annie, she talked about her men friends mostly, a few women friends and of Muttan, who she was in love with. Muttan was in Calcutta, working in a construction company. And she particularly spoke a lot about her boss in office, Raj. I listened to her chatter. I enjoyed being with her for she was ever lively and full of laughter.

I began to take a deep liking for her, and gradually realized how attractive she was. Her laughter no longer sounded that unpleasant.

Annie was very chirpy, caring, and full of energy. Always ready for mischief and very possessive of all her friends. She had a long list of friends and always had a lot to talk about them. But she would go silently red when I made even a remotest mention of my women friends. I found it funny and wondered at the reason of her jealousy and possessiveness when she was already in love with Muttan.

One day, at my apartment, when we were both alone, Annie looked into my eyes and said softly, "Do you know how insecure I feel?"

I was taken aback as I had always seen her in a constant state of laughter and happiness. I looked at her, waiting for her to continue.

"Not many can see how insecure I am deep within. This is what Raj saw in me. He makes me feel secure."

"Annie, I always had that feeling that you were more than attracted to him. But what about Muttan?" I asked.

"Don't know, Shyam. Every person that I meet, I always compare him to Muttan and no one comes even close to him."

"Then why do you have these feelings for Raj?"

Raj was the over-protective type; always advising her and cautioning her not to mingle with new people, and disapproving her long list of friends.

"Because no one has made me feel so secure."

"But isn't he married?"

She turned her head and gave me a silent look.

She was capable of nurturing so many deep affections simultaneously for her many friends, but her feelings for Raj were overpowering and stronger. I could see that.

I reminded myself to ask Annie about something the next day.

1.11

The next logical step was for me to move forward and apply for a divorce.

I had no idea how to go about it. In the yellow pages of the phone book, there were many ads from the attorneys publicizing their services in matters of family law, and divorce was listed in them.

Most ads emphasized that they would do a free one-time phone consultation for up to thirty minutes. I decided to start there, and began calling from the list.

"Hi! I saw your ad in the yellow pages offering a thirty-minutes free consultation and was calling in to enquire about filing for a divorce."

"Absolutely. May I have your name, please?"

"My name is Shyam Venkat."

"Shyam, I'm Frank Rodrigues, and I'm the attorney. Yes, we offer you a one-time free consultation. There is no obligation for you to use our services at the end of the consultation, but I have a great deal of experience in Family Law and can definitely help you."

"Thank you, sir. I got married earlier in the year in India to a girl I did not like, mostly due to my parent's insistence. After marriage, I got a new job, and moved to the US on a H1B-Visa in April, along with my wife. In the first week of June, we got separated when my wife went to live with her sister and her brother-in-law in New Jersey. Our marriage has not been consummated.

"I would like to understand the divorce process, and if I file for it, what are my chances of getting it, given the likelihood that my wife may contest it; and if she does, what would be her grounds to challenge my petition?"

"How long have you been living in California?" he asked.

"We moved from India to San Diego in April this year. Since then, I have been living here. To give a precise date, since 16 April."

"So, you have been here for less than two months. You or your spouse need to be living in the state of California for a minimum of six months, and in the county for three months to fulfill the state and the county residency requirements respectively to be eligible to file for divorce. That's one.

"Two, California is a No-Fault State, which means you are not required to prove your spouse did something wrong. You would state the reason as 'irreconcilable differences' that the law allows."

"Okay, that would mean, I cannot initiate this until mid-October?" I asked.

"Yes, that is correct. Now you said your spouse has moved to her sister's house in New Jersey. I'm not familiar with NJ family laws, but she can file for divorce in the state of NJ if the state's residency requirement is less than six months meanwhile—"

"Okay, my wife will not file for a divorce. When I file one, what are the possible points she can potentially contest?"

"Like I said, California is a No-Fault State. You will get your divorce when you file for it, regardless she contests it or not. I have never come across such a short tenured marriage as yours; and given this, I can't think of what she can contest about."

I felt a rush of relief.

I continued, "Can she lay claim to any of my properties?"

"Have you guys acquired any property since marriage?"

"No, except a car on a loan," I said.

"Okay good. California is a Community Property state. That is, your spouse has equal claim to all property acquired after your marriage. But, she cannot lay a claim on your property that you may have acquired prior to your marriage.

He continued to brief me about the different queries I had, which included questions about alimony and the procedure to send back her things to her. He also recommended taking pictures and a video footage of all her belongings before shipping them back, just as a form of creating evidence.

I thanked him for his consultation as the time was nearly up. He wished me luck.

As I got off the phone, I googled few of the terms he had mentioned. I learned that no-fault divorce represents a modern approach to family law. You won't have to go to court to testify about why your marriage failed. The only thing that matters is that you or your spouse (or both of you) believe that your marriage can't be saved. No-fault divorce speeds emotional healing and courtroom processes by preventing spouses from arguing too much about the inevitable.

I continued my research, and called a few more attorneys. After speaking to a couple more, and being given the same advice, I told myself I had a strong case with a big sigh of relief.

2.11

When I reached office at Mather Square the next morning, I had an email from Aditi.

10 May 1999

So, how are you doing? I guess you must have adjusted by now. And all the good Bangalore habits would have been buried. And it would be difficult to identify you as a Bangalorite. Am I right? Or are you still the same? Some people never change, do they? What else is happening? Appraisals? Anyway, all the best. Go all set to confront and charge. Here many things are happening. So, state of uncertainty in a way. Good, at least something is happening.

    Rest fine.

Bye,
Aditi.

Annie called me as I was reading the email.

"Hey!"

"Da… what are you doing?"

"Edi, wanted to ask you something."

"Ask"

"Edi, so what do I make you feel?" I asked with a sheepish smile.

"I knew that this was coming," she said and started giggling.

She continued, "Raj makes me feel secured, Suresh makes me feel nothing, and you make me feel nice and happy."

It felt nice to hear that.

"And You know something, Shyam?"

"What is it, Annie?"

"You never force me to do anything that I don't like doing. If I tell you that I can't come and meet you, you always say okay. You're so easygoing."

"Wouldn't everyone be like that, Annie?"

"Oh no! That's why I like you the most. You are so very sweet. I like you more than I can tell."

"Yeah? So, how much do you think you like me?"

"I don't know."

"Okay. Give it a try!"

"This much. As big as my little finger," she replied and giggled.

"Trust you to say this," I said.

One Saturday morning, I was woken up from bed by my buzzing phone. It was 4.30 a.m.

"Hello?"

"Hi."

"Jeez, Annie! *Edi, nee enthu cheyyunnu?* It's darn early in the morning!"

"Shyam, I just felt an urge last night to see my parents. Want to go home and decided to take the early morning bus. I need a drop to the bus stand."

"What time is your bus?"

"Six."

"Okay, I will see you in twenty minutes."

"Thanks."

And later, while we were on our way to the bus stand, Annie suddenly leaned forward and whispered into my ears, "Shyam, the girl who'll marry you will be very lucky."

I smiled. And the Cosmic Force smiled.

Unfathomable are the ways of Karma. *Socha bhi na tha.*

1.12

I resumed enquiring with other attorneys. However, I shifted focus chiefly to understand if my situation qualified for seeking annulment or a divorce.

There was a para-legal assistant I spoke to, who at the very outset emphatically replied that I had all the strong grounds to seek an annulment of marriage.

She mentioned that an annulment is granted, under an extraordinary set of rare circumstances. If the marriage was never consummated, or it was coerced upon, or it was a marriage between siblings or between relationships that was not legally recognized; and that I had two of the things going in my favour – coercion, and marriage not being consummated.

I liked the sense of certainty that she provided. For me, this mattered a lot. An annulment was a legal declaration that the marriage is considered null and void, and the person is deemed to be never married. This conformed to my own belief on the marriage, which I never recognized or accepted. Although an annulment vs divorce made no other difference, and a mere technicality; for me, it was the principle of the thing. I was striving for an annulment; it provided a symbolic aptness in the termination of a marriage that I never accepted.

"The good thing about the annulment is that, there is no minimum six months residency requirement to complete for filing, unlike in the case of the divorce petition," she continued. "You only need to meet the county's requirement of three months, which in your case will be mid-July, and you can file immediately after."

I was delighted to hear that. I could file in just forty-five days or so from now. She continued to give me a detailed explanation about the entire procedure, and answered my various queries.

I felt very satisfied at the clarity she provided about the entire process.

I told her that I will provide all information and documents that she needed for the paperwork. Requested her to have them ready so that we can file it as soon as I hit the three-months mark.

2.12

It had been more than a month, and I owed a reply to Aditi. I enjoyed writing to her, and I appreciated that she was trying to keep in touch with me.

17 June 1999

Hi!

My boss Vishal will appraise me. Either he will come down to Cochin or I might go to Bangalore. I am not sure about the increments in this company. I think it is not going to be anything great even for the best of performances. So, I'm not majorly excited about this.

About the 'good Bangalore habits', I tried reading in between the lines. Couldn't make out what you're trying to say. My basic traits have not changed, but otherwise there must be some changes/compromises depending on the place of work. At the end of the day, I still miss the professionalism of my previous company.

What else? Tell me something interesting happening with you.

Bye,
Shyam

Over the weeks, my fondness for Annie had increased. Many a time, Annie teased me whether I too had fallen for her. I had a low tolerance for such frivolous remarks from her. I knew well that I was not going to be another guy falling for this girl. I was sure of being completely incapable of falling for a crazy girl like her. It hurt my ego.

She was sweet but I had grave concerns about her being so insecure. Annie was a person who bonded with anyone emotionally at the drop of a hat and got very close to them. It didn't matter to her if they were total strangers. That single aspect was enough for me to not consider the prospect of marriage. And each time Annie teased me thus, I got ticked off that she should imagine such an absolutely improbable scenario.

My work turned hectic. Karun assigned me a new responsibility. I was to manage the billing operations.

Billing operations was not a glamorous job. It was in a mess. There were numerous complaints from subscribers that they could not pay their bills because they did not receive them. That was the constant feedback we heard during the collection drives from the big-ticket customers. It was initially managed by Customer Service Operations. The Circle Head, in view of the high number of complaints, made a strategic decision that the responsibility of printing the bills and ensuring timely delivery to the customers reside with the Collections credit team. Our credit team had no prior experience of running this. It was a very IT and technical oriented process.

Karun told me, "Shyam, you have just recently moved from the head-office, and your hands-on experience in Collections is still limited. I was debating whether I should make you responsible for Cochin Collections, or make you the Head of Billing Operations.

"After much deliberation, I have concluded that you need to have more experience before you can manage collections on your own. Therefore, I'm challenging you to streamline the billing operations. More than 30% of our customers don't receive their bills in a timely manner."

I was inspired as well as hurt. Hurt that I was being relegated to a task that no one wanted to touch even with a barge pole. Inspired, because it sounded like a real big pain point to the business, and I probably had an opportunity to make a difference.

I was given to manage a team of two analysts, who had been working in billing operations for more than a year. They knew everything, and I knew nothing. My first challenge was in building a relationship with them; and earning their respect.

Amidst my work, it was very refreshing to hear from Aditi.

12 July 1999

Nothing interesting is happening in my life as such. Yup, there is some change in professional life. My boss is now posted at the Bangalore Office. He gave me that long lost resume recently and I couriered it the same day. I don't think you can use it anymore, since it is outdated. But then, it was yours, so I mailed it to you.

So, update it now and then float it. Take precautions. Make sure the local HR does not get the smell of it. Not everyone is nice like us. Rest is the same.

I am planning to go on leave. Will be back on the 19th. If I am not wrong, you are a Cancerian. Wish you a very happy birthday whenever it is. When is it, by the way?

Bye,
Aditi

I was aware that Aditi liked me, and that doubled my likeness for her. I was an email person and relished writing rather than talking on the phone in general. I greatly enjoyed writing to a few people, and Aditi was one of them. I was touched that she had taken the trouble to send my resume. She didn't have to.

I replied, and thanked her.

Two days later, Aditi sent another mail to me. She was leaving Pune.

1.13

Iremembered I had not sent Padma's stuff and I had been procrastinating. I typed out an e-mail to her.

14 July 2003

Subject: Per your request

Hi,

Been busy. There has been a lot of work at office as well.

After our conversation, I went around the house to identify your things. Could you send across a detailed list of your things so that I make sure I don't miss anything when I send them to you, sometime after the coming weekend.

Shyam.

She replied with an angry note the same day.

14 July 2003

Hi,

If you think you are insulting me by asking me the list, you can think that because I don't see a reason why you would want my saris lying in your house.

It will be troublesome for you to see the things of a person you can't stand. In fact, I'm helping you forget me although I know you are a heartless person with no feelings.

Like a fool, I kept thinking things might change and guess what, you win and I lose. You succeeded in getting rid of me without any resistance. Your strategy worked, man. Hats off to you.

The list of things is

1. *My clothes. (There are few on the rack, my saris. Few of my dupattas are in the middle small shelves.)*
2. *The gods (silver ones) and other silver items, except the big lamp which is yours.*
3. *All the utensils and mixer except your coffee filter.*
4. *My books*
5. *My CDs*
6. *My toiletries in the bathroom and a few of my undergarments.*

I guess that's all and if I have missed out anything, I know you would be happy to send it across to me. I think I must return your diamond necklace, my thali, and a few gold ornaments your family had given me. I will be sending them with my mom to India so she can return them to your parents because I don't think it is safe to send a diamond necklace through mail unless you want me to. Although I won't be responsible for it. I don't intend to keep anything of yours.

Oh, you can say you touched me. I feel like burning myself for that. Since I can't do anything about it. Thanks for getting me into such a position where I need to think about telling you what is mine and what is yours.

Padma

I was not trying to insult her, so I made a reply to clarify my position.

15 July 2003

Hi,

About me asking for the list, the intention was to not miss out on any item that belonged to you. Nothing less, nothing more. Just wanted to say this much.

Shyam

I was troubled by what she said, and felt a short email was insufficient. I didn't want her to think somehow in this, I succeeded and she failed and allow her to have that thought, and cause her more pain than I had already inflicted.

I followed it up with a longer e-mail.

16 July 2003

Hi,

I wrote this email and have been debating a hundred times if I should send it or not because I'm not sure if there is any point in it. But you have said so many things about me that I felt you should know yet another time about what I'm going through.

Like you and like everyone else, I too had a million dreams about my life and about marriage. But I never even imagined that I would be in a position like this. My life is equally shattered and I have been as much affected as you have been. I feel frustrated and depressed at the turn of events and see that there is no point in existence. Everything is lost and I no longer see any purpose to lead a life on. It has become meaningless and blank.

I have been reading and re-reading The Mahabharata *several times and have the same question what the Pandavas had every time they went through a period of sufferings – 'Why should this happen to me?' Perhaps, you might have the same question in a different form.*

I'm mentally and physically exhausted now. Physically, because I'm on a punishing schedule, managing both home and work. And I never wanted to be in the US, you know. It is such a lonely life. Sometimes, I tell myself that I need to move on in life, but it isn't easy. I think I will never find peace with god for what has happened and what he has done.

And I'm pouring out my heart because you feel and say that I have 'succeeded'. I don't have anything to say if that's the way you look at things.

I think all that I have succeeded is in getting convinced with each passing day that this life is meaningless and empty. That there is no point in existing for everything that is all around us is all maya – an illusion.

If not today, I'm sure some day you'll be able to look at the whole situation in a maturer way and understand what it is to feel the way I feel by stepping out of yourself.

Someday, you will.

Shyam

2.13

28 July 1999,

Hi!

How are you doing? I am going to Delhi for good on Saturday, so let me say bye to you. You can get in touch with me on 011-6075525 in Delhi. I will send you my mail id later. Rest fine. Wish you lots of luck.

Aditi.

28 July 1999

Hi, Congrats! Do you have a hotmail id?

Take care,
Shyam

28 July 1999

It is aditinarang@hotmail.com or aditinarang@yahoo.com.

Aditi

29 July 1999

Dear Aditi,

Have you got an offer elsewhere? Decided to leave all of a sudden?

Shyam

29 July 1999

Yes, there is something on the cards. No, it is not exactly sudden. It was due for quite some time. I had been thinking about it. I finally decided after talking to my parents in Delhi this time. Anyway, everything happens for the best is my belief.

   Rest fine.

Aditi

29 July 1999

When is your b'day? Will miss you.

Shyam

30 July 1999

The 1ˢᵗ of July. Share it with Lady Diana!! And many other interesting people! Cancerian! Share the sunsign with some nice nuts like you.

   You would have no reason to miss me. You will still be mailing me, understand that? Only my mail id would change. If typing a few letters would mean not writing at all, then I don't know. Rest fine.

Bye
Aditi

Within a few days, I received an email from Aditi informing me of the new company she had joined.

4 August 1999

Hi!

I have joined Esser Telecom India. There is so much to do. It is exciting and challenging. How are you?

Aditi

I was busy with work, and my mind was distracted with thoughts of Annie and I had not written back to Aditi.

I went about methodically studying the billing process, from the basics and studying the flow in action. I asked many questions with my team. I learnt that BPL placed its entire subscribers into five billing cycles each month; and thus, the volume was distributed evenly across these cycles. There were two cycles in the month beginning on the fifth and eight, one in the middle on the 15th and two towards the end of the month on 25th and 28th.

During each cycle date, once the final billing file was provided by IT electronically, my team pulled those files using UNIX commands and directed them to the two heavy duty Xerox printers we had. The printing of the bills completed in two-three days, depending on what issues that we ran into like running low supply on toners, jamming of the printers, prompt repair of the machines by the service technicians, or the flexibility of my team in doing a night duty.Until I took charge, the turnaround times were not robustly measured upon; and hence although the expectation was to complete in three days, it was never met. The team took more than a week just to finish printing all the bills. But, I held my team accountable for ensuring a wing to wing completion of printing the bills in two days or three days at the most. The courier agents were expected to come on day four to pick up the bills for delivery.

Each bill ran into a couple of pages, due to itemized billing with both incoming and outgoing calls being printed. I observed the bills were couriered in their original A4 size. That seemed to be the norm in the industry.

My first success was in achieving timely printing of the bills and dispatching them. I had cut down the completion time for bill printing by more than 50 percent.

There was no magic here; it was doing simple things starting with simply me having a sense of purpose and undertaking the task with a missionary zeal; holding the team accountable for performance, inspiring them and applauding when they did a good job; being tough on them when they erred; and engaging with the vendors closely to have adequate stock of the toners.

The bills that belonged to the rest of the state were sent to the local BPL branch offices and the local courier guys picked it from them for the last mile delivery. I had created a process where the branch managers had to send a written acknowledgement of the totals bills received at each billing cycle, to ensure that nothing got missed from the Cochin office to the different branch offices.

With this, I had earned Karun's respect as well of the other senior leaders in the company. I had become a hero – a newbie who'd come to the circle office and made a mark. Some of my ardent skeptics became my admirers.

I had set a gold standard in managing billing operations.

There were still a few occasional complaints of bill non-delivery that got escalated to me via Karun. It prompted me to push forward to the next wave of my crusade in revamping the delivery process on which I had a very strong gut on how to go about.

1.14

Padma wrote back.

16 July 2003

Hi Shyam,
I really don't know what to say. I think we have gone over these a million times and yet it has got us nowhere. I know you too are not happy, nor am I. It's about us. Not to be blamed on anyone.
I made the decision to go ahead with marriage. You decided to give it a chance. It's not to be blamed on god or your parents. It's about us understanding our differences. Adjusting, sharing and enjoying our life together.
Probably at the end of all this, two things can happen.

1. *You and I will never get along well and go on with our own lives.*
2. *You and I might end up really understanding each other so well although our start never went as smoothly as it should have.*

And you and I know what I want. I want the second one to happen and I want to look back at it and want to laugh about how stupid we both were.

There are things that can happen now. If I come back, I will still be looking for a job. I'm studying and I would be able to write the exam in a month's time if I'm able to concentrate. I'm not able to and that's the reason it is getting postponed.

I still love you, but I need something in return, that's all. Like a little appreciation, affection, respect, and probably, a little romance.

I know you'll be thinking that this girl will never understand me. It's not that I don't understand you. It's about you to stop blaming and indulging in self-pity. It's about you accepting the fact I'm your wife and nothing can be done about it.

It really depressing when you say you don't like me, and you're not attracted towards me. I like Salman, Amir and Madhavan. Does that mean I will wait till I get someone like them? They are just movie stars. What do you know about the kind of people they are? Do you think you would have gotten a more beautiful wife or a person to match your expectations? Do you know for sure she would have taken care of you? Do you know she would not have fought with you?

I don't like fighting with you. Just recall when I have fought? Was it when you were insulting me? Or when you had avoided me or had stopped speaking to me? I know you want your own space.

Ultimately, I know I want to spend each day with you, every minute, every second loving you and having a family.

I think I have told you this, my sister is a doctor and she has a good understanding husband. But they fight like mad. I'm seeing it now. I have seen my parents fight. They have *their inconsistencies in opinions and have arguments. But that does not mean they end up in separation. They are living and working things out helping each other. Taking interest in each other's welfare. Forgiving each other. This is marriage.*

I want you to share your feelings with me. I don't want to talk about you not liking me and my torturing you. It's history. I want us to cross that and go ahead. Then only will any change happen.

I'm ready to come if you think any change might happen. I want you to call me and tell me, 'come let's try working things out' and I will be on the next flight.

But you still must assure my parents because things are not the same anymore. I'm ready to start all over although it's not easy. You also have not been a good person. It won't be easy to forget whatever you have said to me. It's just a matter of time, that's all.

So, it's our lives and our future which we should decide. We are not kids anymore. If you still think I'm not mature, I cannot help you any further.

Hope to hear from you. Let me know what significance this mail holds for you.

Padma

I didn't want to reply to her email. She was still harboring great hope that I'd reconsider and call her back. And any further conversation will continue to go in circles.

When I was making dinner that night, Padma called me several times, but I did not attend to her calls. What would I say?

The next morning, I received an angry outburst from her.

17 July 2003

Hi Shyam,

I know you were home last night but you did not pick up my calls. You are asking me to act maturely, but are you? You might have decided to remain silent, but you just can't. You must deal with me. You just can't avoid talking to me. What a coward you are. I can't just sit and wait that one day you will call me and say I have changed. You think I'm mad? Enough of you just beating around the bush. It's high time you face the reality.

Anyway, I think it's better you send my stuff back. I don't really see anything changing in you or your attitude.

You keep telling me I react violently. Tell me how Radhika would have reacted to a husband like this. No one will just sit around allowing him to do whatever he does and listen to whatever crap he says.

I have had enough. I don't want to sit and waste my time hoping, 'Oh my husband will change. I will get my husband back.'

As you said things have gone too far. Tell me what is in your mind and I will end this. Have had enough of waiting and expecting. There is a limit.

So, tell me what you have in mind and this time you don't have forever.

Padma

2.14

For whatever reason, the bills were all delivered using different courier agencies across the state. There was no one big courier agency that serviced the entire state, and hence there was dependency on more than a handful of agencies, which made it challenging in monitoring and supervising them. I firmly believed that when it came to delivering to each nook and corner of the state, the courier agencies did not have the knowledge and familiarity of the last mile geography as the Indian postal system did.

I bounced off my idea with Karun and Akshay as I embarked upon my plan. Akshay had just gotten back from his medical leave.

9 August 1999

Dear Karun, Akshay,

In the last one month, we focused our efforts in minimizing the billing errors and ensuring 100% delivery of the bills to the

*branches. Towards this, from billing cycle 5 Jul 99 onwards, we
have been able to achieve 100% delivery and we have a written
confirmation from the branches on the same.*

*However, if there are complaints of non-receipt/delayed
receipt of bills, then it is a clear indicator that the final step of
delivering the bills to the customers from the branches needs to
be streamlined.*

*The purpose of this mail is to invite your suggestions/
viewpoints on the postal mode of dispatch. My strong feeling
is that given the explosive growth in the subscriber base, only
the postal department would be competent and more reliable to
absorb such huge volumes. (No one to beat the local postman!)
However, I get to understand that the Kerala Circle attempted it
earlier, but was not successful. If this being the case, I wonder as
to how Credit Card companies like Stanchart (4 lakh subscriber
base) and Citibank (10 lakh subscriber base) rely on the postal
system.*

Kindly share your experience and thoughts on this.

*Thanks and regards,
Shyam*

I had not heard back from either Karun or Akshay, but I figured
it was a good sign. They didn't try to stop me from finding a
solution and I took it upon myself to accomplish it. For the
next one month, I worked hard, made multiple visits to the
Cochin Head Post office, meeting the senior superintendent
and discussed the challenges faced by us. I shared with him
my conviction, that only the postal system could do a superior
job, and asked him for his suggestions.

I told him, I was never fond of the A4 size of the bill, and
if I worked to reduce it, would it even make a difference to

the postmen in the ease of delivery. He jumped on it and said it indeed would, and not just that, it would also make a huge difference at the time of sorting. They had antiquated cupboards/racks with pigeon holes at their departments that they used for sorting. The A4 size bills would not fit in to the pigeon holes, but a reduced size would.

I called up my vendor that printed the billing covers, and told him I needed two reduced sizes for my next bill run, and was running a test. It turned out to be a great success.

I sent a note to the Circle Head and all the Functional Heads.

29 September 1999

Subject: Facelift with a cost cut!

One night, we were racking our brains to figure out the reasons for the supposedly unsuccessful delivery of the bills through the postal system. We narrowed down to one criteria which we presumed could be a major influencing factor towards successful bill delivery – the 'size of the bill'.

We went ahead and decreased the size of the bill cover and introduced two new sizes which are around 50% and 75% smaller as compared to the original one. This was to make the bills appear slim, neat and handy and to facilitate greater convenience of the handling of the bills by the customers, courier agencies and the postal department.

So far, we have received an encouraging response on this from our credit team members and they have confirmed that it is indeed helping them in faster delivery.

To top it all, the new versions, on an average cost 0.50 paise less per cover. Around 15,000 bills were generated this month. Extrapolating this for the entire year, this would result in a cost savings of at-least Rs. 90,000 on an annual basis for the company.

Thanks and regards,
Shyam

My team and I received accolades from the Circle Head, Customer Service Head and from other business leaders from the company. Karun Menon was awfully proud of me. I felt great.

Few months passed. I had gotten very attached to Annie. Lately I was feeling that I was not getting enough of her. The fact that she stayed in a women's hostel was a huge constraint.

She didn't have a cell phone. The only way I could talk to her was at her work number during the day, or at the hostel number. But, calling her at her work number was a strict no-no. The hostel line stayed open only from 6 p.m. to 9 p.m. After 7 p.m., the hostel line was extremely difficult to get through. And when I did reach her, the phone line was on a clock, only a conversation lasting up to three minutes was allowed. After three minutes, the phone line automatically disconnected.

On the weekends, she usually went to her parent's home in Kottayam and took an early morning bus on Saturday, returning on Sunday evening before 7 p.m.

And when she did stay back at Cochin on the weekends, she had a lot of guy friends to socialize with, and to go out with; and I was not the only one. I was never sure where I ranked up in her list of guy friends based in Cochin.

Two days before the Christmas, I dashed to the Archie's Card Center at MG Road.It was already 8.00 p.m. and shops closed early in Cochin. The next day morning, I called her sharply at nine.

"Hi Annie"

"What's up?"

"Edi, I want to meet you for lunch."

"I have a meeting"

"Please. It is important."

"What can be more important than my meeting?" she giggled.

"Very funny. Please."

"Where?"

"At my apartment. At twelve."

"Why at your apartment?" she asked in a naughty tone.

"Simply because it is closer to your as well as my office, and convenient instead of meeting in a restaurant. No worries, you can go back to work by one."

"Okay!"

I went to my apartment ten minutes early. And five minutes past twelve, Annie rang the door-bell. I opened the door and welcomed her.

Annie walked across, staring into my eyes. I could not make out what was wrong with her. She looked disturbed. In fact, she looked angry. I ushered her into my room. She sat on my bed across me without speaking a word.

She asked, "Why did you call me?"

I smiled and waved the greeting card and said, "Happy Christmas."

She took the card slowly and began to read it.

"Dear Annie,

Each adventure, each moment spent together,

fills me with beautiful, magical delight....

And all I can think of is,

how you have made our friendship so very beautiful and that...

Because of you, we are friends forever....
Merry Christmas and Happy New Year,
Shyam."

On the card, I had written 'U are the most lively, naughty, generous, interesting, bad, sweet, dumb, and attractive person that I have met!'

She looked deeply into my eyes. I asked her why she was so quiet.

She replied, "My eyes speak a lot."

Saying that, she came closer and planted a gentle kiss on my cheek, and placed the card inside the envelope, and tucked it carefully into her purse. She looked again at me and asked, "Now, will you drop me back to my office?"

She knew it, but I did not. The fact that I had fallen in love with her.

1.15

25 July 2003

I got two large cardboard boxes from Costco. Before I began packing, I videotaped the house, opening the cupboards in the bedrooms, drawers in the kitchen, pulling them out as I moved the camera focusing on Padma's shelves. Then I positioned the camcorder on a pile of heavy books stacked on a table, and adjusted it so the lens had access to the entire room and started to pack.

While I was packing, at regular intervals, I turned the camcorder on to record the progress and document the list of items I was putting in the box. I wanted to have some proof of the items I was returning, in case she contested that I didn't send her things back.

After a few hours of work, I was done. I walked around the house twice to make sure I hadn't overlooked anything, and that all her items were accounted for and packed inside the boxes. Of her many items, her books were very important as she needed them to study further and to prepare for job interviews. They were very expensive in the US. I went over her list mentioned in the email, and looked at the bookshelf to be doubly sure.

Next, I went around the house videotaping the cupboards, shelves, closets, bedrooms to show the house with Padma's belongings removed, and zoomed in the camera to the box to show what was inside the box.

Satisfied, I taped the box firmly and called Vamsi.

He said he'd be there in an hour. I had already given him a heads-up that I needed his help to carry the boxes from my second-floor apartment to the car. When he came, we both lifted the boxes, carried them, and put them in my car. I thanked him profusely, and drove to the Fedex office at Kearny Villa CT.

I didn't inform Padma that I had shipped her things. On the following Sunday morning, my phone rang. I let it go to the voice mail. It was Padma's mother. She left a polite, long message urging me kindly to call her back, saying that she had an important thing to discuss, while informing that she had just arrived at New Jersey from India.

I was in a dilemma. I had to call her back out of respect and courtesy. But what did I have to offer her to her pleadings? I wrote to Padma the same night, making a weak attempt in trying to stall the meeting, while acknowledging her mother's call, and asked her what it was. She replied it was an important matter that her mother wanted to talk to me offering no details, and urging me to do so at the earliest.

I was torn reading her email. Her parents had been very kind and gracious, and amidst all this drama between us, they had not rushed to interfere. They had maintained a very dignified silence with me.

In deference to her mom's wish, I had to call her. But what would I say if she asked me to take Padma back in my life. I had nothing to offer.

So, I decided to write a letter to her mom, and to everyone detailing the events what had gotten us here. Hopefully, they would be able to understand me better through this.

I started to write.

Dear Athamma, Uncle, Adarsh and Anita,

The purpose of this letter is to communicate the series of events that took place before and after our marriage, which I think that you all should know now, especially after the last episode that happened on Sunday before Padma left for New Jersey on the 4th of June. Most of it or much of what I'm writing down here, Padma may have already told you.

My only request while you read this letter is to remain objective, otherwise you may never get a chance to know exactly what had happened before and after our marriage and that gap would never be mutually beneficial.

Athama and Uncle, our first conversation took place after Mrs Sridhar introduced us. I was in Bangalore and we had discussed to exchange the personal profile along with the pictures of your daughter and mine with one another. And we immediately did. After receiving your daughter's picture and other personal details, I didn't respond as I was not interested, and the next day, as you knew, I went to Delhi for a training program for a week.

When I came back from Delhi, I was contacted by you and Mrs Sridhar asking that I make a trip to Chennai with my parents to see your daughter. I didn't consent to, because I didn't want to go forward with this alliance. It was only when you came down to Bangalore and requested for a meeting again, did I agree to meet.

I was very hesitant and apprehensive in the meeting, considering that I was not interested in the alliance and hence felt the meeting was redundant. Nevertheless, I okayed to meet because of the repeated request, and learning that your family was already camping in Bangalore for the holidays.

(Additionally, I had spoken to Mr Sridhar, conveying to him my initial apprehension about meeting you all as I was not interested in taking this any further. He suggested that it was perfectly okay to meet as one can make a full assessment only after seeing the individual in person and then take a final decision.)

Mr Sridhar also filled me in that you were returning to Chennai as scheduled on the Sunday night, but Padma was staying back in Bangalore at the Sridhar's house and I was to meet her there.

On that Monday morning, I met and spoke to your daughter. I spoke to her for about half an hour. I took this time to make sure I was correct in my decision. The other reason for me taking so much time talking to Padma was because I was served breakfast alongside and took time to finish it.

I went back to office, and the next day morning, I promptly called up the Sridhars and told them I wasn't interested as I didn't want to keep it hanging or provide any false expectations. I didn't want to sugar-coat my response, but instead conveyed my disinterest clearly.

The reasons for not being interested in the alliance could be one or many and these are completely personal and private. I was startled when the Sridhars persisted in asking me the reasons for my decision.

Since that day, when I conveyed my disinterest, the Sridhars contacted me a few times, repeatedly asking me to reconsider. They had got in touch with my dad separately on their own.

I was subjected to heavy pressure by my dad to say 'Yes' and agree to this alliance. Finally, he forced a 'Yes' out of me, and the 'Yes' was something that I said at the spur of a 'weak' moment as I was subjected to several weeks of emotional pressure from my dad asking me to change my decision. It was a one-second moment where I momentarily lost my senses and I hold myself responsible for saying an 'Yes'. Within a matter of few hours, he conveyed my decision to you, and the engagement dates were finalized the same day. It was scheduled to be held in ten days.

Immediately after that, I went to the Chinmaya temple at Indiranagar. I cried and prayed to god to help me as I got pushed into this. And from the very next day, I started pleading with my mom teary-eyed that I didn't want the engagement to take place.

But the preparations for the engagement were underway already. My mother was counseling me that things would be fine, and we cannot afford to cancel the engagement.

Yes, I knew as much, that the engagement arrangements were kick-started based on my word, regardless that it was forced out of me. So, I took some responsibility, and knew that I had no moral authority to call this off unilaterally on my own, or walk off, but hoped to exercise influence and persuade Padma to see reason and get her consent for the break-up. That was my thinking.

I felt helpless.

On the day of the engagement, I was feeling so low in life. I was feeling extremely depressed and unhappy. I remember

Padma crying to my cousin sister that I hadn't talked to her with any love or affection. And since that day, almost daily, I have been lamenting to Padma as to how unhappy I was with the whole arrangement and the way I was forced into the engagement.

I also told her at one point of time, that I didn't feel attracted to her and I wouldn't be happy and didn't want to get married to her. Often, whenever she called me, I would plead that the wedding could be stopped if we both worked together on it.

From the day we got engaged and till marriage, and even after marriage you can check her phone and mobile bills, she was always the one who would keep calling me every day and almost all days, our conversations would not go beyond me telling her that I didn't want to get married to her. Most of the times, she just cried and repeated the same line saying that even if I didn't love her, it didn't matter to her as she loved me, and she would do anything for me that I ask, excepting one thing of not wanting to marry her.

She always repeated these lines, but never was an attempt made to understand what I was going through, and what I meant.

She gave me an emotional threat that she would commit suicide if the wedding was stopped, and she could not take yet another failure in her life for she already had seen one, when she got laid off from Satyam Software which she was not able to come to terms with yet. I felt helpless when she said that.

All the while, the only reason I kept pleading with her to work together in stopping this marriage was because of the moral commitment I felt for the so called 'Yes' that I had said; but for it, I would have just unilaterally called off the marriage by talking to you both, and would have just not presented myself on the day of marriage.

The emotional threat on her part and the feeling of moral commitment prevented me from taking any decision without her consent. Finally, she forced me to get married, and this was just the beginning. I got to see what Padma was really like.

Ever since we landed in the US, there has been four episodes and instances where she's picked up fights with me, spoken to me extremely rudely, been super aggressive in her tone, voice, behaviour and body language.

In one instance, she picked up the phone and made a phone call to her sister and then to Adarsh, sobbing all the while.

When I started to explain to Adarsh what was happening, he held out a threat that he would use all his power to make my life miserable, mentioning that the legal system in the US is very strong.

While I wasn't attracted to her to begin with, I feel extremely repulsed now by her continued display of terrible attitude and behaviour during all those episodes. She has repeated this again and again, though every time, she apologized and promised that she wouldn't repeat it.

While I understand this is a manifestation of frustration and disappointment of a young girl like her, I don't have the fortitude or strength of mind to take such outbursts from her, especially when I had already made it clear to her that I didn't want to get married to her, and she was the one who pushed me into this. I can't go on forever like this.

My life has already ended. It ended even before we got married. There is no charm left for me in it. Both of our lives have been affected now for all the faults that have occurred, nothing can undo what has happened to both of us.

Regards,
Shyam

I wasn't sure how I would send this letter to her parents; they didn't have an email id. Aside Padma, I had only Adarsh's email address in their family. I had to mail it to her father at the India address, or send it to her mother at the New Jersey Address.

I called my sister.

"*Akka*, I have written a long letter detailing the sequence of events from the very beginning. Apart from Padma, no one in their family has heard my version of the story.

"This, I hope will make them understand me, and see what is happening in a new perspective and not judge me as being a mean and sick bastard."

"*Thamba,* no matter what you say, they are not going to be able to empathize with you. Their daughter is in distress, and her life has been turned upside down because of you. And you are the one who is saying that you cannot live with her. You are the one who wants to get separated. You are the bad guy. I don't see any use of you sending a letter to them. It's not going to change how they feel. Maybe your re-kindling the whole thing in your letter makes things worse, creating greater distress and pain to them. What has happened, has happened. Just lie low. Don't send the letter, it will not help anyone. Be happy, *ra*. Focus on your work. Exercise daily. It releases happy hormones."

Radhika's advice made sense to me. And remembering Paresh's woes, I felt an added reason not to send the letter, and avoid creating any unnecessary documentation, that could potentially be used against me.

I made a final decision not to send the letter, nor call her mother back.

2.15

I was surely infatuated to her; attracted to her. I always wanted to be with her, but had not realized that I had developed deep feelings for her, and fallen in love with her.

That was a moment that Annie had dreaded – of me falling in love with her someday. Another beautiful friendship that she cherished, and held so close to her heart would take the turn of love and end the friendship. She read the card again in the privacy of her room in the night. It was with mixed emotions. She felt nice reading what I had written. Yet it made her anxious.

She began to see me less frequently although she continued with her daily half minute calls.

For me, the pain was unbearable. It is a very hard thing to handle when there is an abrupt change in behaviour from the girl that you've developed strong feelings for. I could not understand why she had begun to avoid me lately.

I thought about it long and deep and I decided to tell her what was in my mind.

I told her that I wanted to meet her for just thirty minutes to say something; but she wouldn't oblige, despite my repeated requests. I was not sure if I would even get audience with her. So, I decided to pen my thoughts in a letter.

Annie went for computer classes in the mornings and went to work directly after that. I planned to meet her at the computer class center and hand her the letter.

But I did not want to be around when she read the letter. I planned to give her the letter, and quickly run away from the scene. I decided to dress up in formals with a tie, hand the letter to her and make an excuse that I was running late for a presentation.

Annie stepped out of the class. She was quiet and had the same silent stare. I didn't speak a word. She observed me dressed smartly in formals. I took the letter and handed it over to her.

My voice was shaking as I spoke, "It is 9.10 now. I have a presentation to make at 9.30, so I need to go. I just wanted to give you this letter."

I wondered if she had any idea what the letter contained. She looked angry, and hurt. As she opened the letter, I turned and walked away from her.

1.16

Padma's things were finally delivered on July 31st. I took a print of the tracking shipment details for documentation.

The next day, I called up Karen and told her, "Karen, technically, I have met the county's three months residency requirement on July 17th; so, can we proceed forward to file?"

"Shyam, thanks for following up on this. I'm pulling your file and have the estimated costs. Let me read it for you."

After a few moments of silence, she spoke, "My fees is $775 for preparing the petition for you. The Court filing fees is $227.50. And the total is $1002.50.

"You need to pay me 50% of my fees in advance for me to start working on yours, and in a week from then, I will be able to get all your paperwork ready, draft a petition for your review, and file it in the court. The balance amount you can pay me within thirty days."

"Sounds good. Can I pop in to your office today? I will hand over the check."

2.16

Dear Annie,

In the last few weeks, I find that you have been drifting away from me. I will always respect your feelings, but that it had to happen amidst the strengthening of our friendship has left me amused and wondering.

This would not have affected me, I guess, had I not become extra attached towards you of late. This I know is wrong and dangerous because for any meaningful relationship, there should be a mutual reciprocation.

I better address this issue before it goes out of hand. I have arrived at this decision after a great deal of thought. Remember, I rarely take impulsive decisions. So my request to you is to stop calling me henceforth for some time and instead just speak once in a week or fortnight. I would require this buffer period to appreciate the other good things in life and get back to my normal self.

Do forgive me if I had hurt you in any way. This is all that I wanted to say to you in the thirty minutes I had asked for. I can't wait any longer. I was burdened with these thoughts and just wish to be relieved by letting them out.

If at all, I leave Cochin before you do, I will surely meet you and speak to you. Sincerely hope that you'd do the same. In case you wish to write to me, you could do so at shyam@ rediffmail.com. Cochin is a small place and we might bump into each other by sheer accident. Let's not forget to acknowledge each other gracefully and leave.

Please do forgive me if I'm unable to take your calls.

Take care.
Will miss you.
Shyam

Back at work, I was unable to focus. I kept looking at my cell phone. I was certain that Annie would call me after reading the letter from her office. Forty minutes later, there was a call. There was no number flashed. I did not pick up the call but let it go to the voice message. But no message was left. I knew that poor Annie would go berserk. I was going to be determined and not answer her call. I knew that Annie must have been shattered after reading the letter and would continue to call me repeatedly until I answered. I told myself that Annie would have to understand my inability to talk to her. Gradually reducing the interaction on my part with her was the only way for me to get over her. I wished Annie would understand this.

1.17

1 August 2003

Padma called me that evening. Despite having asked for a signature confirmation, the boxes were left at the door. I was anxious to know if she received them, so I answered her call, to her surprise.

"Hello"

"Hi Shyam," she greeted me warmly.

"Hi Padma, I had Fedexed your stuff. Did you receive them?"

"Yes, I did. We were out of town and when we came back, we found the two boxes at our door. Both my sister and brother-in-law were very impressed how well the boxes were packed. They were huge."

"Okay." I was happy to hear her acknowledge my hard work.

She continued, "You know why I called you? Don't worry. I'm not going to ask you to call me back. I have found a job through Adarsh's contacts and the client employer is ready to do my H1B processing. I called you to just tell you that. Soon, I will have a job and I will be working. I will also not be a burden for my sister, by living here and not paying for my expenses."

I was delighted to hear that for two reasons: one, that she seemed to have accepted the inevitability of our separation, and two, if she got a H1B Visa, the annulment proceeding I was going to start would not have any adverse impact on her ability to stay in the country. She was on a H4 dependent visa currently, which meant she was authorized to stay or live in the US, only so long as we were spouses. And she would lose her eligibility to stay in the country when we got divorced.

I felt that US would be a far better place for her to be. Leading a life as a divorcee in India would be far more painful, dealing with negative perceptions from people around.

"Padma, that is great news. I'm very happy to hear this. How are you planning to do your H1B visa? You know, there is the normal process, or you can fast-track it through a premium process, which you will get in fifteen days?"

"It will be a regular processing. The premium processing will be expensive."

"Padma, I can help you with the premium processing. I think it will cost you about $1,500 and I will mobilize that amount for you, and pay you in a few installments over forty-five days, if you will consider doing it? That way, you get your visa quicker, and you can start to work sooner. I will send you the link to an article on this that gives you more details," I said.

"Okay, I don't have a bank account yet. You have to send the check in the name of Adarsh."

"I can do that, but let me know when you are going to file, and what your full processing fee structure is. And can you find how I can send it to Adarsh – by check or wire?"

I wanted to create a sense of urgency, making sure she filed it before I embarked on my petition for an annulment.

We spoke for a while as I was very relaxed, and before we hung up, I reminded her to get back to me.

Padma sent an email to me the next day, telling me the details of the filing for H1B visa and the processing of it.

I replied to her e-mail, and copied Adarsh to loop him in. After all, the payment had to be made in his account.

In the email, I offered to help her with the fee of $1500, although in three installments of $500 each over a period of time. The next day, Padma sent another e-mail, saying she needed a copy of my passport, H1B Visa to enclose them with her paperwork for H1B filing. I was mobilizing funds into my bank account and getting ready to send her the first installment check of $500; but I was bummed at her e-mail.

I was very scared of sharing my passport copy. What if they misused it? I have read horror stories online where the girl's parents have used the information to file a police case of dowry harassment and prevent the guys who visited India from leaving; by black-listing their passport numbers at the airport immigration, or apprehending them upon arrival.

I did my own research, and found the husband's passport or visa information was not required for the H1B processing of the wife's. I shared that information with her. Padma was persistent that her immigration attorney has said it is mandatory. Over the next few days, we were trading email notes, and I was continuing to challenge her attorney's statement, and asked pointed questions to show me, where the USCIS lists it as a required document. Finally, her attorney conceded that it is ideal to have the document in case of a RFE

(Request for Information) query from USCIS, although not a required document at the time of fling. Padma continued to follow-up on it.

I was determined not to give her a copy. I was simply scared. The emails between us became bitter, and finally, I decided to drop the idea of funding the premium processing; for it no longer seemed of any consequence for her, as the entire focus seemed to be on the document.

2.17

It was 12.00 p.m. Akshay had called me for a meeting. I put my cell on silence and left it at my cube, and headed to the meeting room. It lasted for an hour. My mind was not there; all I could think was only about Annie and the call I was expecting, but determined to ignore.

When I came out of the meeting room, I glanced at my mobile. It had not rung. I was surprised. I went out and had lunch. It was 2.00 p.m. by the time I finished. Yet, there was no call.

I had mixed feelings. It was a sense of wonder that she had not called. Now I was no longer sure if the anonymous call had been from her earlier in the morning. At the same time, I heaved a huge sigh of relief that she had not called. At 3.00 p.m. I received a call. I did not want to look at the number that flashed, but picked it casually. It was Sooraj, much to my irritation.

By 4.00 p.m. I had begun to feel a little anxious. Annie had not called me yet. I could not focus on anything. I kept looking at the phone every minute.

"Was she angry? Did she not understand me..." I began to think. My heart ached.

I had had no intention of answering her call just a few hours ago, but now, I was hoping against hope that she'd call me. I wanted to talk to her and hear her voice desperately.

I trembled as I dialled her work number.

"Hello, this is Annie."

"Hi," I said.

After a pause, I said, "I am sorry. I was stupid. I told you not to call me, but had to hear your voice. I am sorry for all that I wrote."

"Heheh," she giggled.

I felt relieved to hear her laugh.

She said, "I finished reading the letter just as I reached the office. I tore it and threw it away."

"Really?"

"Yes, but you were looking good today in your formals for your meeting."

"Yeah, I made that up. I didn't have any meeting to attend," I said.

"Heheh. You looked cute."

"Listen, I want to meet you today. At 6.30 at Bimbis?

"Okay."

I felt a huge burden off my chest. I felt so happy. She was a real sweetheart.

But I knew that if I really had to get over her, I had to move out of Cochin and go to some place far away. Time and geography does help a broken heart. There was no future between her and me. She was engaged to Muttan. And she didn't approve of my affections towards her.

I thanked god when I finally got the appointment letter from GE Capital two weeks later.

1.18

6 August 2003

I knocked on the office door. Karen's assistant opened the door, and took me to her office. Karen showed me the petition that she had prepared.

I read the document.

I, SHYAM VENKAT, do hereby declare:

Respondent and I were married on March 8, 2003 and separated on June 4, 2003 when Respondent moved to New Jersey to live with her sister and brother-in-law. During the 2 ½ months we never consummated the marriage by having sexual relations.

I am requesting the court grant me an annulment because I was unduly influenced and coerced to get married by my parents, Respondent, Respondent's parents, and by the social customs of my homeland India.

I tried to put off the marriage and I told Respondent on several occasions that I really didn't want to get married to her. Respondent told me that if I didn't marry her, she would commit suicide. This threat of suicide caused me great distress and I was unduly influenced and coerced into marrying her.

After the marriage, we moved to the United States from India. The marriage has never been consummated between us. Since leaving India I no longer feel pressured and under the influence of my parents, Respondent, or Respondent's parents, and I feel free from the social customs of India. I now feel free to correct the terrible error of our marriage.

Because of the short duration of 2 ½ months, and because of the undue influence and coercion I was under, I respectfully request the Court to grant me an annulment.

I declare under penalty of perjury under the laws of the State of California that the foregoing is true and correct.

Dated: 08-06-03   Shyam Venkat
                                          Petitioner In Pro Per

I read it, and it looked great. I found it well-drafted, concise, and to the point. The only piece that was not factual was the mention of Padma's parents pressuring me into the marriage.

I told Karen, "This looks great. It aptly summarizes. However, want to clarify that my wife's parents did not press upon me. So, that is the only edit I have."

Karen smiled, and said, "That's okay. I see your intention. But, we will leave it there. This is merely to highlight the pressure you had from multiple fronts."

I felt uncomfortable about it, but quickly rationalized that maybe it was not a big deal. I felt good to note that Karen had mentioned the pressure from my parents, and had kept it honest.

I signed the document, and drove back home feeling happy that I was moving forward to seeking my freedom.

Karen filed the petition the next day. She sent a copy of the filed petition to Padma by certified mail to her NJ address, with a signature confirmation. She repeated it was critical that Padma was notified of the petition, and a proof of signature confirmation had to be presented in the court before we could request the court for a judgement date.

"If Padma refuses to accept the document, then we will have to send it by a Court Bursar. That will cost a few hundred dollars more," she said. "Let's see what happens."

I was worried, but there was nothing I could do, but hope for the best.

More than a week passed, when Karen called me at my home and left a message. I called her back.

"I have got some good news to tell you," she said.

"Tell me Karen! What is it?" I asked eagerly.

"I have a signature confirmation from your wife! She received it on 14th!" she exclaimed.

"Wow, really. I can't believe it!" I shouted in Joy. I didn't expect it would be this easy.

"Yes, this is great! Now, she has thirty days, upto September 14th to respond. After that, we will file a motion for a judgement date with the court. The court will provide a hearing date. On the day of the hearing, you will come to the court and answer any questions the judge poses. And that's it."

I later learnt from my parents, to whom Padma mentioned that she had joyfully accepted the certified mail, thinking I had sent her the installment check for her H1B premium processing. When she opened it and read the contents, it came as a huge shock to her. She was brutally mad at me.

I got hate e-mails from her. Her family was shocked to know I had initiated formal annulment proceedings in the court. It was a bombshell. The news spread like wildfire among my family members too. There was a flurry of phone calls to me – from my uncles, cousins urging me to re-consider. Padma was in constant touch with my dad, and a few of my cousins, pleading them to instill some sense into me.

Just as I was nearing the thirty-day mark, Karen called me on the 12th at my office to say that Padma had responded to the petition to the court directly, and her response was dated the 8th. The court seemed to have received it in the morning. She said she went to the court and collected a copy of her response. And she asked if she could swing by at my office to hand over the copy.

When I met her outside my office lobby, she looked visibly agitated.

"Shyam," she said, "It appears that your wife did not send the adequate court filing fees with her response. If that is the case, then the court cannot officially accept her response. I'm double checking this information, and waiting to hear back from the court clerk. It is also possible that your wife has subsequently sent another response with the correct filling fees, and the court is yet to receive."

"Okay," I said slowly.

"Anyway, I wanted to keep you posted, and give you the copy of her response regardless. I will keep working my phone line to the court clerk. In any case, the court must receive her response with the right filing fees latest by 14th, in another two days, that is. If at all, they still receive anything after 14th, it will not be entertained."

I did not understand completely how her response or lack of response can potentially impact my petition for annulment.

Perhaps, she could contest my grounds for seeking annulment; I wasn't sure about it. I was tired to probe further, and just took solace in the understanding that the process will be simpler and quicker if it was uncontested.

"Okay, Karen. Thanks. I appreciate you coming over to give the copy." I took the copy and walked to the parking lot towards my car. I got in hurriedly, and started to read it.

2.18

I had my first interview with GE Capital International Services, Gurgaon more than five months ago in mid-August. It was well before the time I had fallen in love with Annie.

After I passed the phone interview, I was called in for an in-person interview. When I had flown to Delhi, I went without telling a word to Annie. In those three days while I was away, Annie had left many panic-stricken messages on my cell phone, asking where the hell I was, and if everything was okay. When I returned, I did not tell her the truth. I was afraid that if I ever did, Annie would pray that I should never leave her, and that I should not get the job. I had broken the news the previous evening on the phone that I was changing job and moving to Delhi, and wanted to meet her before I left. I had requested her to give me a handwritten card.

I felt deeply disappointed when I saw her walking with empty hands when we met in the park. We looked at each other in the eye and walked quietly towards the lone bench and sat there looking at the people around, and not speaking much.

I carried a camera with me. I wanted to take a picture of her and as usual, she declined. I insisted one more time and she promised that she would take a very good picture and send it to me.

After that, neither of us spoke to each other. We just blankly stared at the world outside them. After an eternity of silence, Annie took the brown diary that I held in my hand. She flipped through the pages all the way from Febuary 2000 and stopped at the page that read '28 September 2000 Thursday'. She took a pen and began to write. I tried to look as she continued to write.

My b'day – for you to remember always.
I wonder if I am the most crazy
Irritating
Dumb
Fascinating
Understanding
Wonderful
Beautiful
Pal
You've ever had?

When she gave me the diary, I noticed a tear in the corner of her eye.

Annie was surprisingly, extremely composed when I had told her that I was leaving for Delhi. I had not imagined that she would take the news in her stride. I had thought that she would be devastated and shattered. Even if she was, she didn't show any of those emotions. Maybe she had begun to expect that I would leave Cochin someday and had prepared herself.

The deep silence continued.

Finally, I stood up, preparing to leave.

"I will miss you. You take care," I said softly and shook her hand.

In that moment, Annie produced a handwritten card from her pocket and gave it to me.

Goodbye, I'm really going to miss you
I'd like to smile
And wish you goodbye,
But I can't ...
I've practiced, but the smile
Always dissolves
When I think of how it will be not having you around....
...I know I'm being selfish,
But it just shows how important you've been to me
And how very much I'm going to miss you.
When someone as special as you leaves,
They're bound to leave an empty space
Which will be very hard to fill.
But I do wish you well and I will say goodbye...
But don't ask me to smile, at least not yet.

– Linda Lee Elrod

It was signed 'Annie'.

When I finished reading, a tear trickled down my cheek and fell on the card. I looked at Annie. There was a deep pain in her eyes. I whispered, "Bye" and walked away without looking back.

1.19

I, PADMA LAKSHMI, do hereby declare:
PETIOTIONER and I were married on March 8, 2003. We arrived in the United States of America on or about April 16, 2003.

I moved to the State of New Jersey after PETITIONER forced me to leave, threatening suicide if I did not.
PETITIONER received pressure only from his family to enter into this marriage. At no time did I or anyone else in my family put pressure or coerce PETITIONER.

Petitioner mentally abused me during the two-and-a-half months that we lived together.

PETITIONER brought me to this country without a work visa and without a means to legally support myself. I am currently being supported by my sister and brother-in-law.

Because of my circumstances and inability to legally support myself, I require PETITIONER to provide spousal support.

I declare under the penalties of perjury under the laws of the State of California and the State of New Jersey, that the foregoing is true and correct.

Dated: September 9, 2003   Padma Lakshmi,
                                       Respondent in Pro Per

I heaved a sigh of relief as I finished reading it. Padma had not mentioned or contested the date of separation, and thereby confirmed the short tenure of the marriage.

She had also in her own words, confirmed the coercion on me into the marriage. The two strong grounds that I was leaning on in seeking the annulment was being confirmed and agreed by her.

Next day, when I reached home from work, I called up Karen.

"Hi Karen, just wanted to check if you heard of any further response from my wife?"

"Hi Shyam. No, the court has not received anything today. That is a good thing. Just one more day to go, she has no case, so why would she want to spend money on this. But let's see."

"Okay, thanks Karen."

It was 14th the next day. After I returned from work, I was itching to call Karen. I debated about it a few times, and then decided, I would wait till the next day afternoon, and that way, Karen would have the updated information as of the close of the business hours of the court.

15 September

I walked into an empty conference room after finishing lunch. I closed the door and dialled Karen.

No sooner did I say, 'Hi' she raised her voice in excitement, and said, "I have got great news. Your wife did not re-send a response with the filing fees. So, I will make a motion to the court, seeking a default judgement hearing."

I was happy to hear. "Thank you, Karen! This is great to hear."

"We are getting closer. I will keep you posted. I will file it tomorrow. You are not required to sign any papers for this. And from there on, we will have to wait for the court to respond and provide a hearing date. I will keep you posted."

"Okay, sounds good. Thank you, Karen," I said.

2.19

February 2000

It was a cold Friday night. There was a bit of unease in my heart. A new job in a new place far away from home combined with the melancholic thoughts of Annie made me restless.

I stepped out of the airport and looked for a placard carrying my name. There were hordes of people with their heads and bodies thrust forward on the iron railing. I spotted a stout old man with a long, flowing white beard in a yellow turban holding a sign that read 'Shyam – GE Capital'. I waved at him and the old man picked my luggage and led me to his cab.

I sat down quietly.

The pain of unease continued to remain. It was Annie on my mind.

Over the flight, I had a chance to think more clearly. Annie had Muttan. And her love for him seemed evergreen. And she was such a crazy girl, not the kind that I would want to marry. Despite being aware of it, I had such strong feelings for her.

I quietly resolved to let my mind off her. I would use the huge geographical distance created between us as my ally, and to my advantage. I wished her happiness in life. And I asked for happiness for myself from god.

But little did I know, that the Cosmic Force was going to give me just one of the two things that I had asked for.

Unfathomable. *Socha bhi na tha.*

1.20

A month passed. During that time, Padma's father and mother visited my parents at our house in Coimbatore. They came to give back all the jewelry we had gifted to Padma during the wedding. And my mom returned the jewellery that they had given. Her father and mother had cried inconsolably, joined by my mother. My dad continued to counsel optimism with them, assuring that he'd talk to me, and get me reunited with Padma.

Her parents were extremely kind and acted with grace. They didn't abuse or shout or scream at me, unlike the many episodes that I had heard where it gets bitter and ugly.

My dad continued to persuade me to re-consider and take Padma back.

One day, Karen called me to say the court hearing had been scheduled for January 3rd.

I was happy to hear it, but it was happiness combined with anxiety. I had to appear in the court, and answer any questions the judge may have for me. Karen explained that since she was a para-legal, she could only assist in doing the paper work, and coordinating with the courts. But she was not an attorney, and could not appear for me.

I informed Vamsi about it. He was very happy for me.

The day before the court hearing, I asked Vamsi if I could borrow his cell-phone the next day. I told him, that just in case I had an emergency at the court, or needed anything from him or Karen, I would reach out to them from the court.

On the 3rd morning, I woke up, took a shower, and prayed. I had not informed my mom or sister about the court hearing. I had taken the day off. The court hearing was at 9:30 a.m. I reached the court at eight.

I walked inside the court and passed the security check.

I was feeling heavy in the heart. I was bracing myself to be prepared if in some weird way, Padma showed up in the court, to argue against me.

I had more than an hour to kill time. I walked inside the court building, and found my way to the designated court-room. I entered the room, and sat inside to familiarize myself with the court-room setting. A session was in progress, but I could barely hear when the attorneys spoke.

I was worried, what if I didn't understand what the judge said or asked me. How would I handle that situation? I was on my own. I turned restless, and stepped out of the room, and walked up and down the corridor chanting, *Om Namo Shiva* continuously inside my mind.

At 9:15, I walked inside the court room again, and sat down nervously. Five minutes past 9:30, my name was called out and I was asked to stand.

The court clerk read out the oath, and asked me to repeat it.

"I swear by Almighty God that I shall speak the truth, the whole truth, and nothing but the truth."

The judge quickly glanced over my petition, and asked, "Are you seeking an annulment of your marriage?" I had the impression he had already read through it before-hand.

"Yes, sir," I replied, raising my voice so that he could hear me across the hall.

"How long were you married?" he asked.

"Less than 3 months, sir, before we got separated."

"He smiled and said, yours is probably the shortest marriage I have heard of, apart from Britney Spears." There was a wide chuckle across the court-room.

He said, "Granted."

And moved on to the next file.

That was it. I wasn't sure if I heard him right. I walked over to the court clerk and clarified with her the import of his word. She said my marriage has been declared annulled by the court, and I would be receiving the necessary paperwork from the court.

My chanting of *Om Namo Shivaya* increased in intensity. I thanked god profusely in my mind while continuing my chanting, and walked out of the court. As soon as I walked out of the court building, it seemed weird and unnatural to do, yet I mustered all the effort that I could, and jumped up high in the air and shouted "Yay!"

Within a few days, I received the annulment papers from the court.

2.20

One of the first things I did reaching Gurgaon was go through the stack of emails exchanged with Aditi six months ago. I had printed and carried them along to look for her phone number.

I got out of the hotel room and walked to a nearby STD booth. First, I called Paresh and told him about my whereabouts. He had left Stanchart after a year of my leaving and had joined American Express in Delhi. He was very surprised to hear from me. I enquired where he was living and found that he was about forty kilometres away from my hotel. Too far to meet often or hang around.

Next, I dialled Aditi's number.

It said, 'This number does not exist'. I walked to the internet browsing center, and emailed her telling about my whereabouts and asked for her number.

The next day.

"Hello"

"Hi Aditii!"

"Heyyyy Shyam! How are you? It was such a pleasant surprise to see your mail."

"I know! Neither did I think that someday, I would come all the way here to Delhi to work."

"Wow! You're here! When did you come?"

"Came here Wednesday night."

"Have you found a place to stay?"

"Not yet. I'm looking around. Currently, I'm in a hotel at Gurgaon."

"How do you like it so far?"

"It is chilly and cold here. But I am glad that I got out of BPL."

"How's everything going at BPL?"

"Much is the same in the Kerala office, but there have been many changes in the Bangalore office ever since you left."

"Yes, I heard of it."

"Shyam, my boss is calling me. What's your number, can I call you back?"

"Aditi, I'm starting work this Monday, and will let you know as I find out what my work number is."

"Okay, do let me know."

"Sure, *chalo*, then!"

"Bye Shyam."

My first day at GE was a day of meet and greet introductions. I met the HR leader Kavish Sarkar who gave me a high-level overview of the private label credit card business in US, Collections Operations at GE, and walked me through the company's organization chart.

The India Site leader was Ravi Sharma. His leadership team consisted of Collections AVPs – Kush Malik, Jyoti Singh, Sangeeta Das, Shailaja Puranik who managed different delinquency buckets across the various client portfolios, AVP-Dialer Operations, AVP-Compliance Head, AVP-Six Sigma Quality, AVP-Transportation & Logistics, AVP-HR (Kavish), and Collections Risk Strategy and Reporting team. Kavish introduced me to some of them, who were at their cubes and offices.

Later, as he walked me to my designated cube, he mentioned that Uppal Mathur was another recent hire into the Collections Risk strategy team, and he and I were to work together with a functional reporting to Nancy Dooner at Canton, Ohio USA, with a dotted line reporting to Ravi Sharma.

Uppal Mathur had joined three weeks ago, from IMRB, a Market Research Firm. Uppal was thirty-one and titled 'Manager-Collections Risk Strategy' and I was twenty-four, titled 'Assistant Manager-Collections Risk Strategy'.

Both Uppal and I were expected to work in developing optimal risk-based collections strategies for the different portfolios.

Our task was to support Nancy and her team with analytics to help drive the formulation of the strategies; and since more than eighty percent of the collections accounts volume was outsourced to Gurgaon and Hyderabad, it made sense to have a team based in India for closer engagement with the operations leadership team. So they created these two positions and hired us both to represent them at the India site.

I had never done similar work before. Nancy, who interviewed me, was impressed with my functional knowledge of collections process in the Indian setting. She felt that I would add value, bringing in my hands-on collections experience. Uppal too had not done this work in any of his prior jobs. He was hired for his analytical expertise.

The office had two floors. Each floor was sprawling 20,000 square feet. There was a sea of boys and girls, young men and women working in both the floors.

The teams were organized based on delinquency stages. Customers who had defaulted one to three payments were categorized as soft delinquency and those who had four or more payments outstanding were bucketed as hard delinquency.

Naturally, collecting on hard delinquency was more challenging; and only experienced and better skilled associates were assigned to that process.

It was a stressful job, compounded by having to work in night shifts to keep up with the US time. It was not uncommon to see a few associates muting their phones and yelling at the customers to take the stress out. They were strictly required to be polite even when the customers were abusive or screamed at them.

But the whole atmosphere was cool. A vast number of associates were from nearby smaller towns and cities and they were earning big bucks with just a modest education. They were simply required to converse in English and had to be trainable. The collections skills were imparted upon hiring; and their accent, diction and pronunciation all polished during the rigorous three-week training.

I underwent the same three-week training, as it was felt by Uppal that it would be very educative, and help me immensely in my work; and it was a great way to acclimatize with the collections process in the US.

True to that, I found it extremely beneficial. It was fun too, for I made a considerable number of friends who were all fresh out of college and younger than me.

2.21

I realized that I had not sent my work number to Aditi yet. I emailed it, and wrote to her, that I would call her shortly one of the days as I settled down in the new job.

There were multiple lessons to pick up in the job. There were many things that were completely alien to us, and we were clueless about. It was very overwhelming. We had to get an intimate understanding of the US credit cards business, the collections strategies and procedures, familiarity with the new statistical tools such as SAS and simultaneously focusing on building relationships with the India leadership team and the US team members.

It was a job with a high level of responsibility. I found it to be very intimidating – especially on the part of interacting with the local senior leadership team, for they had sky high expectations from us in aiding their collections performance metrics with our strategies.

Uppal and I didn't know what we didn't know, neither did we have a full idea of what we needed to know. It was all ask and learn. There were no process flow charts, or any orientation material to leverage in doing our core day to day work. Since we were the newly created team in Gurgaon, we didn't have any predecessors locally to turn to.

And the worse thing was none of the senior leadership at Gurgaon site had any inkling about our work. We had to depend on the US team for helping us in coming up to speed, and the geography and time zone disparity made it very challenging.

The local senior leadership team, expected us to hit the ground, not running, but sprinting. We were asked for opinions on different topics, as to why the Collections Effectiveness (CE) was low week over week; what was the expected impact on the delinquencies with the gas price spikes in the US. What did we know? We had just joined, and we didn't know enough, and what we knew wasn't adequate to talk with authority.

The lack of intimate knowledge and familiarity with the business and the collections function made me diffident, and I felt very uncomfortable in the various meetings I attended with the local leadership team. This was not a concern with our US team though, who had a full understanding that we were on a steep learning curve.

Within a month of my joining, the US team created another new team, called it Collections reporting team and hired Sahana and Pratul from outside. Neeta Bahrani moved internally from Operations and joined the reporting team as a third member. They reported to Wally Z in Canton, who was Nancy's peer, and with a dotted line to Ravi Sharma.

There was a weekly staff meeting with all the operations leaders and the strategy analytics and reporting team. Ravi Sharma presided over those meetings. He did a round robin of general functional updates before diving into the main agenda topics.

From the very outset, I found the four of us – Uppal, me, Sahana and Pratul, except for Neeta, were never in his good graces; he didn't think highly of us. He spoke to us in a condescending manner in the limited interactions we had. And thus, I was more intimidated by him.

During the same time, Uppal, Pratul and I made a three-week business visit to US to meet the different team members in our collections strategy and reporting team, across the different GE offices.

During our trip, Nancy announced a new organization structure. She had Ken Marks, Anusha Kris, and Gene Shultz as her direct reports. Uppal was put under Ken Marks who was leading Collections Credit Score model development and validation. I was put under Anusha Kris who was leading Operations Collections Risk Strategy.

After we had returned to India, during one such staff meetings, just as we were walking to the conference room, Uppal asked me casually, to provide a brief update on our US trip, and what we accomplished in those three weeks.

There were about ten or more people in the room. It was a mid-size conference room with the chairs squeezed next to one another forming a circle. There were Collections, Compliance and HR AVPs in the room. Four of the leaders spoke and provided a short update of the prior week's highlight in their respective functions. My turn came to speak. I had not made any mental rehearsal of the points I wanted to say, and started to speak impromptu. After about fifteen seconds, I stopped mid-sentence for I lost my train of thought. I drew a blank and did not know what to say next. There was a brief five to seven seconds' pause.

Uppal was seated beside me, to the right and he instantly jumped in, and continued where I left. In less than a minute, I recovered. As Uppal continued speaking; Ravi interjected and asked a question, and when Uppal finished his response, I pitched in, for I had organized my thoughts by then. And building on Uppal's comments, added more colour to it, hitting on all the right points.

As I finished, Ravi Sharma mentioned that he was greatly looking forward to hearing about our analytics work in the coming weeks and months; and urged us to stay connected with the Operations leaders very closely, and have him updated of the key project initiatives that we undertake. After forty-five minutes, the meeting ended.

The next two days, I went about my work as usual. On the third day morning as I woke up in my apartment, I had a flash of the meeting scene in my mind where I had blanked out for a few seconds in front of everyone. That made me feel terrible about myself. I felt very ashamed. I replayed the whole scene several times.

Over the next few weeks, this recurring thought started to dominate my mind every waking moment. This gave in to a morbid fear of speaking in those weekly meetings thereafter, extending to other speaking situations.

It was the beginning of a prolonged depression that I had invited myself to and it was to stay for years to come. It wreaked havoc on my feel-good and cheerful spirit.

Weekends were especially very painful, as I stayed alone in the apartment, and my mind was consumed with a mental replay of the incident numerous times in the day, denting my sense of self-worth and alongside sharpening the fear of speaking in front of the senior leadership.

Both Uppal and Sahana were married. And Pratul was the lone bachelor, who lived far away from Gurgaon. I didn't get to hang out with them a lot and Pratul was around twenty-six kilometres away which I found difficult to cover on a bike, in the heavy traffic ridden highway. I was like a one-man island.

Wherever I had a chance to visit their homes and spend time with them, it provided a respite, easing the fear and the associated pain. But it was short-lived and returned as soon as I went back to my regular life. Of course, no one in the office had the slightest inkling. I appeared normal, sporting a smile always.

Pratul had asked me once, "Shyam, you are great. You are always smiling. You don't seem to have any worries in life."

I replied with a smile, "Pratul, don't go by the constant smile that I wear. It is deceptive. I have my share of worries!"

No one could see the violent grief behind my smile, except me. Not even my sister, who was very intuitive otherwise and picked on, very swiftly.

2.22

April 2000

I had not spoken to Aditi after returning from my US trip. I had spoken to her prior to the trip briefly, when I had called her, but had been interrupted by Uppal to join him for a meeting. I had told her that I would call her back some other time.

One early evening when I was at work, my phone rang.

"Hi Shyam!"

"Aditi!"

"How are you? How is work?" she asked.

"Nice to hear from you! I was wondering how you were... I had been meaning to call you."

"I have something to tell you. Is this a good time to talk?"

"Ya, Sure....tell me," I said in anticipation.

"Last weekend, a boy came to see me from US. And we had a small, simple engagement ceremony. The marriage date is not fixed yet..."

"Aditi, wow! Congratulations!" I exclaimed, "This is a big surprise! Who is the lucky guy?"

I was indeed surprised at this sudden turn of events. She said there was one small wrinkle in the whole thing – that he was already a green card holder, and that was worrying.

I asked her, "I don't understand. Why is that an issue? Isn't that a good thing that he is on the path to acquiring citizenship."

"No Shyam. If he was a citizen, then there would have been no worries. I would be immediately eligible to apply for a permanent resident card after marriage, and could travel with him to the US. But in the case of a green card holder, the permanent residency is not granted immediately to the spouse, but is subject to the annual caps, and a wait-list. Until I get one, I cannot travel back with him to the US."

"Really?"

"Yeah, it is usually tough to sponsor for immigration for a spouse when you are a green card holder. It is easier, to sponsor when you are on H1B or are a citizen, but not when you have a green card. The only way is I apply for a college in the US and go there on a student visa."

I quietly listened and assured her everything would be fine.

I have had a belief that women stay in touch as long as they are single. Once they get committed or married, there is an eventual decline of interest towards the friendship; with their attention fully re-directed to their spouses and family.

So, I told myself that I needed to brace for the expected – there would be an eventual breakdown in the frequency of phone calls from Aditi. And soon enough, she may not even bother to call or even look forward to receiving mine.

And so, I had completely forgotten about Aditi, until I got a call from her one afternoon.

"Hi Aditi," I said flushed with embarrassment and added, "I'm very sorry. I haven't called you for a while. Work has been very busy, having to fire from all my cylinders, and I had some people visit us from US last month."

"That's okay. How are you Shyam?"

"I'm missing home, Aditi! Otherwise, work is great. How are you? What happened to your student visa?"

"Well, I have got the Visa interview at the American Embassy next month. I'm very worried, hope it goes well."

I said with a smile, "Aditi, all you need to do is wink at the gentleman interviewing you, and your visa is assured."

She laughed at what I said, and replied, "Shyam, that is very flattering! Thank you. I'm keeping my fingers crossed. Anyway, keep in touch. Give me a call sometime. I will talk to you later."

"Okay. Take care."

2.23

Each waking moment continued to be living hell. My mind was paralyzed with that singular thought of a potential speaking situation in front of the local leadership, and it felt like being burnt on a fire, with the heart and the chest feeling heavy, like carrying a weight of hundred thousand pounds. The fear and anxiety was utterly irrational.

Few weeks passed and I had not called Aditi, even once.

One day, my phone rang. I picked it, and said softly, "Hello".

"Hi!"

"Hi Aditi!" I said.

"Shyam, how come you have not called me all this while? Even the last two times, it was I who called you..."

I chuckled and said, "Sorry Aditi! I have this notion that once a girl gets engaged or married, she no longer cares much to hear from her friends."

"How mean of you, Shyam. How can you say this?"

"Okay, tell me when is my treat?" I asked with a broad smile.

"Why don't you come home for dinner this weekend? I will invite Dev as well," Dev was our common friend from BPL, living in Delhi.

"Great. I would love to have home-cooked food."

"I will make a south Indian dish, maybe upma. You are a vegetarian, right?"

Upma did not sound enticing, to say the least; but I appreciated that she was trying to think of a south Indian item.

"Yes, I'm a vegetarian. Just eat eggs though."

"Okay, this Saturday evening at about sixish? I will mail you the address and directions."

"Okay, cool. *Ghar ka khana*, I will come anytime!" I said and laughed.

Aditi's house was in Dhaula Kuan, about twenty kilometres from Gurgaon. I had a bike and rode in it to her house. It was easy to locate her house. I rang the bell.

She opened the door, carrying a huge book in her hand and greeted me warmly. She looked both, beautiful and pleasantly attractive. She looked the same as I had met her the very first time, excepting she looked prettier and fairer now.

I walked inside, and sat in the corner of the sofa, and made myself comfortable, as she commented, "That's a smart haircut."

I thanked her and glanced at her hands. She had a book called *Atlas Shrugged* in her hands. She called out to her parents, and introduced them.

They both addressed me, "*Beta, kaise ho?*"

I was touched by the manner they addressed me. It was a very intimate word of endearment. Her mother made her way to the kitchen immediately thereafter, and her dad excused himself and stepped out for an evening walk.

"How is this book, Aditi?"

"It is by Ayn Rand. It is very interesting. It is about people with opposing ideologies – capitalism and individualism vs socialism. I'm just halfway through."

Her mother walked in, and interjected, *"Kya piyoge, beta? Chai bana lu?"*

I beamed a smile, and said, "Ji aunty!"

Our conversation shifted to my US trip, and my work at GE. After about forty minutes, Dev arrived with a box of sweets.

The three of us spent the next couple of hours going down the memory lane, of our work days at BPL US West, partly bitching about things there. We talked about the politics, mostly enquiring or updating each other about the whereabouts of common friends and colleagues that we had worked with.

We had dinner and followed it up with a short stroll in the nearby navy campus.

"So, Aditi, tell me about your fiancé?" I asked.

She smiled and remarked, "You know, there were three things that I had wanted in my man. He should not be a doctor. He should not wear glasses. He should be very tall. And funnily, my fiancé is a doctor, wears glasses and is not tall enough either!"

Dev and I both laughed.

"So, why not a doctor?" I probed.

"You know Shyam, there are many doctors in my family. What I see is that they don't have a life, and they have no time for the family."

"And how tall is he?"

She replied with a smile, "As tall as me... I can't even wear heels when I'm around him."

"Does he know, how lucky he is to have you in his life," I said, and added cheekily, "Or should I tell him?"

She shot back a warm smile, "Aww, you are sweeeetttt."

We congratulated her and wished her the best, and left after bidding bye to her parents.

I felt good seeing Aditi after a long time; and enjoyed the nostalgia filled conversation with her and Dev. That was my first meeting with Aditi at Delhi. And that would be the last time I would ever see her. And we fell in love. It was not puppy love. It was weaved and embedded in every interaction we had subsequently, but never spoken out aloud in those three words. It happened suddenly and quickly, before both of us realized it.

Socha bhi na tha. Unfathomable are the ways of Karma.

2.24

Five months passed. I didn't give any thought to Aditi. I was happy she was on the path to her new life.

One day, I received a short email from her informing that she had quit Esser Telecom few months ago, and taken up a temporary assignment recently in a software startup company as a hiring consultant. She gave me her new contact number.

I called her on a whim from office. I was curious whether her wedding date had been fixed, and what had happened to the visa interview.

She didn't elaborate much. She merely said that she didn't know if it would work out. She hadn't gotten the student Visa. It had been rejected. And I didn't ask her much as she didn't seem keen to talk about it.

I quickly shifted the conversation to other things. I told her about my work, and what I do in greater detail. I indulged in some light-hearted self-deprecating humour that I'm usually fond of doing with people that I feel close to. Told her how I get constantly ragged by Uppal and Sahana because of my

South Indian English accent, and pronunciation. She listened with amused interest, and gave me a few pointers for my own defence.

One day, I received an email forward of the love story of Infosys founder Narayan Murthy and Sudha Murthy. It detailed how Narayan Murthy had pursued his dreams and started Infosys with conviction and courage against all odds. I was also very impressed at the way he proposed to Sudha Murthy. He had highlighted his negatives – I was struck at that style as I considered that I was capable of the exact same approach in the event I profess my love to a girl. That would be my natural style – emphasizing my self-identified negatives and yet professing my love and affection!

He said the four words instead of the usual three. It felt nobler to me. I wanted to share this with Aditi, and forwarded it to her.

Aditi wrote back, and I was happy to hear that she enjoyed the story with equal zeal.

4 October 2000

Hi!

Thanks for forwarding this to me. In fact, I have already read this about 2 weeks back. Read it, I don't know how many times. It's so very romantic, and something everybody would want to happen and not have the courage to make it happen.

How did you find it?

Aditi

4 October 2000

Hi!

This is a story which anyone can relate to completely. Found it very passionate and touching. Feel that lady luck is another key piece in addition to courage. He dared, but succeeded and that makes the difference.

The other striking aspect is the way he proposed to his wife. Was impressed!

Shyam

5 October 2000

Hi!

Do you have a yahoo id? If not, then make one, if you like to chat that is. I'm 'vela' for a few days till our ad is released next week. So, I'm bothering all my friends who are equally vela or want a change.

Your work must be hectic as ever. What else is new? By the way, are you off today for Dussera? And ya, what plans for Sat? Interested in any movie? Am not sure at the moment though, might have to tag along with my folks somewhere. Will tell you for sure tomorrow.

Anyway, if you are at home, then enjoy your holiday. Maybe check out those restaurants – Centre Point: Kanchi or A.P Bhavan Canteen.

Bye
Aditi

5 October 2000

Hi!

Is your chat id the same? i.e. Aditinarang. Certain chat/mail ids are firewalled here.

Our team is expanding, and we have a new girl joining us next week.

Today the call center is relatively quiet. Not too many people in the floor. Since it is a chhutti, I have come in shorts. Find it relaxing and it is a small perk!

Shyam

6 October 2000

Hi!

Did you see the movie, 'You've got Mail' yesterday on HBO? I watched it in bits and pieces since I had already seen it. I like both Meg Ryan and Tom Hanks, so watched it again. You must catch up with 'Forest Gump' today on HBO.

Wow, your team is multiplying beautifully?

And what else? I'm still not sure about tomorrow. Mom is planning to go out of station for a wedding, so if I can make it and if you happen to be home, I shall call you up and let you know.

And what else? At work? And no cackling in the background. And you in your bare minimum?

Well... well... Don't invite too much attention since you don't seem to be interested in it. Those GE babes are dangerous!

Take care
Aditi

6 October 2000

Hi!

Went to Sahana's home yesterday evening. Had Gin and watched 'You've Got Mail.' Enjoyed it a lot. What time is 'Forest Gump' showing?

So, that means you will get to know only tomorrow. What time?? Give me a call tonight if you can. I have got a phone at home now, number is 0124-47638689.

Have decided not to venture again to the office in the 'bare minimum'. Can't handle the attention!

Hey, do you like chocolates?

Write in,
Shyam

6 October 2000

Hi!

Good to know that you have somebody in the vicinity now. So, you can alternate between gin and rasam once in a while.

I'm not fond of calories coated in brown.

Ya, I shall call you up today or tomorrow and let you know if I can make it.

Bye
Aditi

2.25

I continued to wake up every day, with that pulsating fear, the same that I carried with me to the bed in the night before. A fear of violent proportions that I had never experienced before, or heard of. My mind automatically gravitated to that incident, played it and replayed it a thousand times. It consumed my mind totally, and controlled my life.

I was somehow managing through the meetings and presentations that I had to do on regular basis. I noticed that the initial few minutes of speaking was the biggest struggle I had. But once I was past it, I felt very comfortable and in-fact, confident too. Yet, my mind was fixated on the nervousness experienced in the initial minutes.

I had hoped after a repetition of successful speaking situations, the fear would vaporize away. But it didn't turn out that way.

One such was, where the operations leaders wanted to know, if there were risk differences by states on the collections performance; if so, were they statistically significant.

I made a thirty-plus page deck, laying out the analysis extensively providing a view on different vintages, across different delinquency stages, by portfolios and visually illustrating them with charts. I included a couple of pages for executive summary, where I showed the consolidated performance by each of the fifty states, adjusting for the accounts volume, highlighting the key takeaways at the bottom of the slides.

Before I began my presentation, I handed over the hard copies to the operational leaders who were assembled in the room along with Uppal. Seshadri Raman, AVP, Quality flipped through the pages quickly for a few seconds, and remarked smilingly in half jest and half seriously, that he was already impressed with my analysis, feeling the weight of the deck, as he lifted his hand to gesture it; and that he had never seen such a bulky deck, and was looking forward to my presentation.

I spoke, beginning with an overview of the purpose of the analysis, and the data used for it, explaining the observation vintages and the performance period data.

Then, I jumped into the meat of the analysis, taking few minutes to familiarize them with the charts, and how to read them; calling their attention to the trends observed across the portfolios and due stages for the different states.

Through the presentation, I was interjected multiple times by the different leaders with questions, or seeking clarifications and I answered them with ease.

Finally, I called their attention to the summary pages, and I concluded that the key takeaway was - 1) There is definitely statistically significant differences in the performance by the states; 2) When viewed in isolation, I said, calling out a bunch of low volume states that had very high delinquency rates that one would potentially conclude that these are the worst performing states, that needed focus and prioritization in our calling efforts – "But".... I made a pause for effect.

And I resumed, "...that takes us to the 3rd takeaway, which is, we should not look at these states in isolation. Instead, you need to weigh it by account volume and then do the comparison. For example, although MD is off the charts with the highest delinquency rate of 26%, its relative account volume contribution is a mere 0.5%. On the other hand, NY that has a high delinquency rate of 16%, not anywhere near the 26% of MD; but it drives 28% of delinquent account volume and 35% on delinquent dollar exposure.

"So, in this table, you see I have added a new metric to the extreme right, which is the delinquency rate multiplied by the relative volume contribution and ranked the 50 states in the descending order of this metric.

"When you look at performance in this manner, the high-risk states are your usual suspects – CA, FL, NY, NJ, and TX – the high-volume states, and it is these states, we would want to focus on our collections efforts if we wanted to spin the files in the dialer based on state risk to make an impact."

My presentation was well received, and the leaders were very appreciative for the insights. I was on the top of the world that evening as I walked out of the room. Later when I rode back home, I chanted *Om Namo Shivaya* continuously in my mind, feeling grateful.

I told myself that this is akin to getting back to form in cricket. I was back to my natural game; and good riddance to the paralyzing and irrational fear. For the first time since that incident, I experienced a prolonged sense of joy and euphoria that night and hit the bed, feeling happy and blissful. That feeling lasted, bulk of the next day, and alas, after which, it erased completely. Back to square one.

I found it difficult to establish a pattern for my nervousness. There were some occasions where I felt totally comfortable; and in fact, eager to speak when I was placed in front of a friendly audience. And on other occasions, where I perceived the audience to be hostile or intimidating, I found it extremely stress-inducing, to put it mildly.

I experimented enrolling into dance and guitar lessons to check if these activities eased my mind. The dance helped a bit, and I found myself completely absorbed in it when I practiced.

2.26

On one Sunday morning, my phone rang, as I came out from the shower.

"Hi Shyam"

"Hey Aditi!"

"I wasn't sure if you were up on a Sunday morning, but just thought I would give it a try."

"I just came out from my shower. I woke up early."

"How was your Saturday? What did you do?"

"Nothing much. In the morning, I went for the guitar class, with Paresh and Sahana's husband, Sridhar. And I went to work for a few hours in the evening.'"

She laughed and said, "Somebody is learning new skills to woo the women in the office."

I beamed, and said, "Aditi, I think wooing a girl is easier than learning guitar!"

"So somebody has a lot of experience in these matters!" she laughed.

I laughed and said, "Yeah....it isn't easy at all. I have been going to the classes with lot of excitement, but I'm just not getting the hand co-ordination right. The instructor has gotten tired of teaching me, that he has already shifted his focus on the other two pupils who are very promising."

"I'm sure if you set your heart and mind to it, you will learn it," she said.

I chuckled, "I have realized passion is one thing, but skill is another. And the lack of even an ounce of success is testing my motivation in continuing with the classes."

"Don't give up that easily...," she said teasing.

"Talking about not giving up, did I tell you about my sense of dressing?"

"Now, what about your dressing that you are going to tell me?!" she asked in amused wonderment.

"I used to be a big fan of Allen Solly brand. I had a pair of dark yellow trousers that I wore on a regular basis. I had a friend in MBA who had a great sense of style. He made so much fun of me saying he had never seen such a pair of trousers in his life. And asked me if I would take it off and give it to him. He found them irrresistable.

"I merrily laughed at his dialogue delivery; yet it never made me aware about what a lousy sense of dressing I truly had. And now when I think of it – OMG, why did I wear such crappy colours. In fact, would you believe I had purchased those yellow trouser for my sister's wedding reception and had worn them?"

"Ha ha... I hope you still have those yellow trousers?"

"Ha ha ha... I wish I had given it to him the first time he had asked. And not made a fool of myself by wearing it so many times."

She laughed heartily, and asked, "So, Mr Rainbow that you have been, do you have any snaps in the orange shirt and that yellow trousers?"

"Why?" I asked innocently.

"I can send them for Govinda look-alike contests!" she said, and laughed.

I joined her. I then heard her mother's voice calling her in the background.

"Okay, I will let you go, Aditi. It must be your breakfast time."

"It was nice talking to you. Ok, I will catch up with you on email tomorrow."

"You too, catch up soon," I said, smiling happily.

Aditi didn't have a cell phone, nor did I.

It was an unspoken agreement between us, that she would be the one always calling me in, rather than me calling her home, and run the frequent risk of her parents answering the phone. I was alone in the flat, sharing it with no one, and anytime was a good time for me to talk. And along with the occasional phone calls at work, we were keeping up with our daily emails during the week.

I greatly relished her sense of humour, and her witty rejoinders to the things I said.

I discerned she was forming strong attachments towards me; and found it surreal that I could attract the affections of an extraordinary girl like her, despite me being an ordinary guy. At one level, I was enjoying and looking forward to talking to her, waiting for her daily emails in great anticipation, savouring the things she said and wrote, replaying it mentally several times thereafter during the course of the day at work, and smiling and chuckling while writing a reply to her.

At a different level, I was wrestling at the end outcome; where this would take us? Wrestling with my sense of low self-worth, that I was not worthy of her. She deserved someone better, a person more superior than me. At the very minimum, a person not hijacked with such an irrational fear of public speaking. I adored her; wanted to marry her; was in love with her, but the Damocles' sword of fear hung over me. It didn't let that feeling of love that was in my heart to be sanctioned by my mind, but instead constantly reminding me, that I, in my current condition of mind, was simply not worthy for her.

I thought of it many times, though poor Aditi had no clue of what was running in my mind.

2.27

I walked into the conference room with nervousness. Ravi was assembled with his direct reports. The VPs of 2 due stage collections, 3 dues stage collections and 4-7 dues collections were seated. The dialer Operations VP was present too.

Uppal, Sahana, Pratul and I were seated in adjacent seats. I was working on a project with Anusha to execute a test by matching strength of the Collector's Skills – high, medium and low and their varied effectiveness in working on low risk, medium and high-risk accounts as a proof of concept.

When my item came up in the agenda, I rose. I was not required to do a stand-up presentation, but I relatively felt comfortable standing up and talking, and stood wherever it was feasible and the meeting setting permitted.

The room was dimly lit, and my power point page was pulled up on the giant screen. A dim lighting always helped, for it eased the nervousness that I don't get to see people's faces. I was allotted ten minutes.

I started to speak, and a slight tremor accompanied my voice.

"This is a high-level update on the Collectors Skill Test that I'm working on with Anusha. Currently, at the collections floor, the dialer throws the delinquent accounts on a random basis to the available collectors. It is done regardless of the risk levels associated with the accounts, or the skill levels of the collectors.

"What we are proposing as part of this test design, is to

1. Segment the delinquent accounts into three broad categories based on their collections credit score – High risk accounts, Medium risk accounts and low risk accounts.

2. Segment the collectors in each shift based on their combined last 6 months performance into 3 categories – Best Collectors, Medium Collectors and OK collectors."

By now, as I continued, all my nervousness disappeared, and I became confident, and was at ease.

I said, "If you would look at the illustration on the right, this proposal is to send high risk accounts to the best collectors, send medium risk accounts to medium skilled collectors, and low risk accounts to Ok Collectors. And test if this approach delivers statistically significantly higher collections.

"Again, we want to test it as a proof of concept. We recognize there are quite a few operational challenges in executing it, and Anusha and I are working with the collections leaders Kush Malik, Sangeeta Das and Shailaja Puranik to iron out the operational execution challenges to mitigate any bias into the test; and in ensuring the test is carried out in a seamless manner in the floor, being transparent to the collectors.

"We plan to test it for a period of thirty days, and then we will go back and analyze the data and report the findings," I said.

Everyone was listening with great attention. This was a new thing that they had not heard about before. I was feeling great, for I was at absolute ease walking them through the two pages, and was enjoying presenting it to the group.

Ravi however was skeptical and challenged that it was going to be very tough in executing the test from an operational standpoint.

I acknowledged his concerns, and mentioned that again was the intent of this test to scope out the level of effort, operational feasibility, viability of implementing it on a sustained basis aside the analytical results.

When there were no more questions, I sat down.

Sangeeta Das tapped on my shoulder, and said, "Shyam, thank you. That was an excellent presentation."

I felt great, and happy, and smiled back a thank you. I had a euphoric feeling for the remainder of the day.

But the next day, when I woke up, the same piercing fear and pain returned. I was disgusted with myself, that I could muster no power to control it.

2.28

"Hi, busy?"

"Hiii Aditi. How was your day?"

"Pathetic Shyam, although my role is hiring, there is a hiring freeze at the company. The budgets have been slashed, and we are not hiring until next year. So, I'm vella, and no work, so decided I'd bother you."

I laughed and said, "Enjoy the free time while it lasts. And when it gets busy, you will miss these days. My work is similar, go through a cycle of hectic work and plenty of downtime, it keeps alternating; but averages out in the end!"

"Why is that?"

"Since my work is project based. We are supporting our risk management team in Canton, so we work on the adhoc-analytical requests that they send. They reach out to us based on their needs. We have plenty of downtime, but it is not unusual, sometimes, these come as urgent requests with tight timelines," I said and asked, "You know what Anusha said last week?"

"What?" she asked with interest.

"Manjeet had joined our team recently. He and I were on a conference call with her last Friday night. We were discussing an analysis that she urgently needed. When we presented it to her, there were some follow-ups, and she said very sweetly, 'Shyam and Manjeet, can I ask you both a favour? Since you are both single, can you please work on Saturday to finish this for me? You can take the Monday or some other day at your convenience off to compensate. This way, I will have a Sunday to put together a presentation based on your data and analysis, and present to Keith on Monday that I'm scheduled to meet.'

"What could we tell her, but I told myself, 'Anusha *behn*, at this rate, we will continue to be single if we work on the weekends like this," I laughed.

Aditi laughed along too.

"Anusha is visiting us next month for a week," I said. "This time, she wants to spend a few days touring around."

"Where are you taking your Anusha dear?"

"She wants to go to Agra to see the Taj."

"Ah, you are taking Anusha to Taj via-Agra?" she asked with a gentle laugh.

"Yes, via-Agra!" I giggled.

"Your parents must want their son to be married, before he embarks on such trips via-Agra?" she asked.

"You know, Aditi. There was a time, when my father acted very strangely. It was completely out of his character. This happened three years before, at the time I had joined Stanchart. A family friend of ours checked with my dad that her daughter and I would make a great pair."

"Hmmm," she said. I sensed she was listening keenly.

I continued, "They were family friends and we used to meet frequently and they would visit us at our house. I have seen this girl who is much younger to me. My dad was insistent that I consider marrying her. I was not interested at all. I was spooked at his persuasion as he has been a cool dad, giving both me and my sister plenty of liberty and freedom.

"Why did you not want to get married to her?"

"Well, I was too young to get married. Had just started my career. And more than anything, I didn't find the girl beautiful. And Aditi, honestly, her mother was more beautiful compared to her daughter," I said and laughed.

"Chhee chhee chhee," Aditi said in mock disgust, but didn't utter anything else.

"Finally, I told dad that I see the girl as my sister. And that was the clincher. He stopped persuading me."

"That was smart, Shyam. Was your mom supportive of you?"

"Yes, both my mom and sister were. They agreed with me, that she was not the right girl, she had just passed her boards. And neither was there any hurry for my marriage. I hope my dad does not talk about such things again when I go home—"

She swiftly interrupted me, and asked, "When are you going?"

"Planning to go in early December."

"How long are you going to be gone?"

"For the whole month. Plan to return in January."

She went silent. I sensed she would miss me for that entire month.

"Your parents and sister must be thrilled about your vacation," she finally said. "Do you have access to Internet there?"

"There isn't one near our home," I said, "But I will be in touch with you through e-mails, when I get to an Internet café," I offered a vague assurance, without any specific promise.

2.29

Our daily e-mails continued, and our phone calls that were occasional earlier during the week at work, turned frequent.

We had moved to a different building, 22A in the second floor and our seating arrangement had changed. I was seated next to Neeta, and Sahana was directly behind her and diagonally across me. I was in her direct line of visibility.

She had to just turn her head slightly, to look at my back, or at my screen.

She called me for her usual smoke break one morning.

"Shyam, whom are you talking to every day and for so long?"

I tried to brush it off, saying that it was a friend.

She persisted, "Which is that friend to whom you show all your 34 teeth?"

She had nick-named me as '34 Teeth' in her same-time chat, implying that I keep laughing all the time showing my teeth, and the number increases to 34 teeth when it is a girl.

"Tell me, I know it's a girl. Don't try to hide anything from me."

"Why don't we talk about something else?" I asked.

"No, you have to tell me now," she snapped and looked at me.

I was caught off-guard, and was in a big dilemma. I have shared some key secrets or episodes of my life with her, including the irrational fear and anxiety that I was going through.

But this one, I was hesitant about. Simply because I believed in keeping such a precious thing, of the love between us, to myself for now until it firmly crystallized. Not to utter a word, or speak of it to anyone, until then; else I worried, the magic would be gone.

Anytime I consciously applied my mind, and thought of Aditi, I had always felt dazed. It was plain unfathomable. *Socha bhi na tha.* Dazed that she entered my life abruptly, dazed that someone so wonderful and precious like her, could even fall in love with me, dazed that I had the love of a woman who I wanted to marry, dazed that requited love was such a rarity.

Dazed that I was charmed by her in multiple ways, I was turned on by her ready humour, and her clever witty retorts, her diction and eloquence and at her immaculate English, the natural grace in her speech and thoughts as a matured woman, an attractive listener, a vast rarity; she who smiled and teased me often where she could, that I relished greatly; she was thoughtful, and caring; and beautiful in and out; in appearance and in heart!

Which ordinary looking man, with nothing extraordinary about him, gets lucky like this?

This was a divine occurrence, and it merited all the sacredness associated with a sacred secret. I did not want to be frivolous and talk about it to anyone; not yet.

Looking at my reluctance, Sahana said, "Shyam. You are so young. Don't make the mistake like Sridhar, falling in love at a young age. You have a career to focus on. You are just starting with your life – you're hardly twenty-four years. You must create a strong financial net worth for marriage. A heart of gold is of no use in matters of marriage; a girl will expect, rightfully so, some basic comforts and luxuries and you have told me, you don't have much of a bank balance, and that you are helping your brother-in-law with money, who is struggling to find a job.

"You will meet a lot of interesting people along the way. You will be more mature to take the right decision. This is not the time to fall in love. You are doing great in this company. Everybody respects you. They consider you and Uppal as the analytical brains. You have a promising career ahead of you. Don't screw it up with these distractions," she said strongly.

"Who is this girl?" she demanded again.

I found it difficult to hold back, and gave in. I told her about Aditi. She was surprised that I had not breathed a word about Aditi, all along, despite having shared with her other things that were very personal.

She shot back, "Are you in love with her?"

"It is complicated – yes and no."

"Why?" she asked.

"Yes at the heart level, but a no at the mind and intellect level."

"What are you saying?"

"Well Sahana, I told you about that incident. That continues to give me a shitty feeling. I still go through that pain and fear every day."

"What are you saying? I thought you are past that now. Didn't I tell you, that it was such a trivial incident; no one noticed it. In fact, for someone like me, who prides in having a strong memory of things, even I had forgotten about it until you told me. Shyammmm, do you realize that it is nothing, only you are making demons out of it?"

My face turned pale, and I gave her a pleading look that I was helpless.

"Shyam, you are being plain stupid. You fought like a lion, you spoke so well after that brief pause. You made some great points. Stop beating yourself like this... don't be crazy and that is why, I tell you, you are so touchy!" she said.

She continued, "Now get out of it. Coming back to Aditi, I don't believe that distinction at mind and heart level you made. It's simple. Either you are in love, or you are not in love. So, you are *not* in love with her. If you flip a coin, and ask yourself, if you are truly in love with Aditi, and don't say Yes before the coin lands, then you are *not* in love."

I said nothing, but her words continued to ring in my mind.

The immediate impact of which was I didn't reply and write back to Aditi the whole of that day, and the next day, and broke for the very first time, the sacred and unspoken pact of daily email exchange on weekdays that was on a glorious run for months.

Aditi wrote to me on the third day, after I had gone silent on her for two continued days.

Hi!

You really are busy or revengeful because I kind of expected your mail. You know it happens, if you get something regularly, you kind of start expecting it. Guess I should not take you for granted. No, I have not exactly done that, only probably your mails, yes. Expect them every now and then.

And what else is happening? You'll be rolling out your plan tonight with Anusha? I'm sure you are geared up for it. (No pun intended, so don't try finding one! Naughty mind that you have.)

Don't work too hard. It will show when you go home. Your sis might be impressed with your biceps but not with your health in general.

Rest tomorrow, but you can always write in.

Aditi

I was torn with guilt during those two days of my silence; cursing myself for my behaviour. I was beyond happy to see her sweet innocent email that was devoid of any drama, or harsh accusations of any kind.

I could not resist a moment longer in holding back a reply. I immediately started to type at a furious pace, offering an apology that I was busy at work; fully recognizing it was such a lame line considering the cardinal sin I had committed.

2.30

Few weeks passed. And my trip to Coimbatore was fast approaching. My mind and heart was dulled with the same pain, fear and anxiety, thickly laced with a shitty feeling of myself; and a deep sense of low worth.

But I had my tasks cut out at work. Since I was to be gone for a month, I had to bring to closure many analytical projects that were work in progress before my vacation. There were a few additional projects that were given to me ahead of time, simply because there would be no one to work upon in the following month.

I was happy to take on all that extra work on my plate, being grateful that Anusha was so kind to let me take a four-week vacation, something especially unheard of for the US team members.

I worked longer nights, leaving office late, and came to work earlier than usual.

I prepared myself, for what now seemed to be inevitable. I could not let this dilemma of my future with Aditi linger, if I was not totally with it.

On the pretext of hectic work prior to the vacation, I cut down on the long phone calls with Aditi and suggested to her that we just continue talking through the daily emails. She was a sweetheart, very empathetic with my work situation, and agreed.

I had booked my ticket on the Rajdhani Express to Bangalore. The train journey was about 34 hours long, and I'd reach Bangalore in the morning. Radhika worked at Bangalore and stayed as a paying guest. My brother-in-law lived in Chennai, taking care of his parents, who were old, while continuing his search for a suitable job.

Radhika had planned a two-week vacation coinciding with mine to spend time with me, and she had booked for us both to travel the same night to Coimbatore by Conti Travels.

My train was on the 30th of November.

27 November 2000

Hi!

I'm making sure that I carry the GE travel bag (to flaunt in the train!) – what else to do for those long hours? With the logo and the name splashed all around! But the flip side is, GE is immediately associated with a Collector's profile and even if someone were to ask what the job is and I briefly tell them about 'risk & collections strategy', I have a feeling that they should be thinking, 'Bechara! He can't even manage a Collector's job!'

Didn't Shakespeare say that a rose would still smell the same even if it were called otherwise? On the contrary here, we are made to believe that its all in the name! What else would one say of this – Mr local boss in a bid to recruit for his reporting/

MIS team, went to naukri.com and searched for a 'MIS' profile and guess what, we have one Mr. 'MIS'hra who has joined us! Well, just kidding! Planted this joke today, which made the entire team including Mr MIShra burst into laughter!

How's the day going? Yet to get over the 'Monday morning blues'?

I felt jealous when you said you were walking up and down the lawn! Forget the lawn, I don't even have a cactus at home!

So, when your brother is here in Dec, are you saying that your shopping list to him has a strict no-no to all those calories coated in brown?

Take care.
Write in.
Shyam

27 November 2000

Hi!

If the idea is to flaunt your portfolio and attract attention, then I think that festive dress, your well-earned biceps and somewhat expert hands at the guitar would do the job better. You can sing your way through to Bangalore and for all you know even make a few bucks in the process. Isn't that real value for money?

You can actually do gardening on your weekends. Stand in the balcony, water the plants, gape at the neighbours; some might volunteer to help.

Monday is quieter than expected. It's drizzling outside. Guess ther'll be snowfall in the Himalchal hills. Right time to go to Vaishno Devi, wish I could extend it to some sight-seeing in Jammu, but guess there won't be any time.

I don't think I can afford too many chocolates and I don't think my bro would get too many. Even if he would, half of them would be passed on to our cousins as small gifts.

Nothing major. Small-little jobs, newspaper and surfing should take the day through.

Click some snaps in the evening with the gung-ho crowd so that your sister would be rest assured that you would not go single on your next holiday.

Bye
Aditi

27 November 2000

Hi!

The idea of making those extra bucks is quite tempting and the fact that it's going to be totally tax free is all the more! Will think of the gardening bit once I come back!

I finished my six sigma black belt certification today. Feeling good about it. Have you heard of Six Sigma?

What else? I need to book my return tickets today. Work is just the same. Inching forward. There will be lots of calls to attend to in the evening.

Bye,
Shyam

28 November 2000

Hi!!

How was yesterday evening? What time did you finally go home?

Which calls are these? And could you book your tickets yesterday?

Yes, I know about Six Sigma. My general knowledge is not as bad as my financial condition.

What is new there? Write in. Was not the weather lovely yesterday? Did you go out yesterday?

Bye,
Aditi

I reserved a cab to take to take me to the Nizamuddin station. The train was at 8 p.m. I asked Aditi if she could come to see me off at the station. She said it would be difficult to get out of the house that late, with her parents being conservative. She would try, though.

I hoped against hope, that if she did, just seeing her in person would provide me with immense strength and overcome the self-constructed nasty feelings, and surrender to her my inner afflictions and in the same breath, profess my love. The last time I had met her was under totally different circumstances; and I had looked at her just as a dear friend.

Now, my heart yearned to see my love; and this was a great pretext to ask to meet and see her.

She however couldn't make it and was very disappointed.

She asked me to keep writing to her, and said she wasn't asking for my home number at Coimbatore for she didn't wish to bother me, during my time with family. And if possible, I could call her at her work or home, when I could. I had kept the expectations with her at the very low; telling her I had no easy access to internet cafes and that my emails to her would be sporadic.

And neither did I protest when she refrained from asking for my Coimbatore home number; nor did I make any pointed response on being suggested that I could call her.

I was going to use this time away from her, and miles away from Delhi to assuage my feelings. I had reached a decisive phase in our relationship where I had to take a stand and go forward. I had to say I love you and I want to marry you or I had to put a stop to this, if I reckoned the overpowering shitty feeling about myself was continuing to numb my senses and spirit.

I was already massively guilty of prolonging this, despite being unsure of being able to marry her, yet creating hopes and expectations in her mind that it was merely a matter of time, I was going to be proposing to her. And say those magical three words or the four words. In my mind, if I did that, it would be the four words with her, and not the three words. The four words were the superior and subtler expression of the depth of love I felt for her.

It was a battle between the beats of my heart, and the sounds of my mind. My heart wanted to pursue this relationship into holy matrimony, but my mind was playing the devil's advocate, of speaking against it.

2.31

I reached Bangalore. Radhika came to receive me. She was so happy to see me. We took an auto to her paying guest room. It was a one-room house with an attached bath. She had a small stove that she used for easy and quick cooking; otherwise she ate outside.

Immediately after we had breakfast, I gave her a stack of emails, and told her,

"*Akka*, I have known Aditi for a while. She is a Punjabi girl, and is from Delhi. My ex-colleague from BPL whom I met the first time at Pune. I want to marry her. Rather than me describing her in length, here is a stack of the emails we have exchanged. You read them, and you will get to know her. And tell me, what you think."

Radhika was visibly surprised, for until then, I had not uttered a single word about Aditi.

Later that evening, we went out for dinner, and boarded the night bus to Coimbatore.

As the bus started and thirty minutes into it, Radhika spoke, "*Thamba* I read all the emails. Aditi is a very nice person.

But Amma will be heart-broken if you marry a girl outside our community. Already, Amma is saddened with what I did. And you see, love marriages seem to be jinxed in our families. Look at my own, or Pratima *vadina's* or Sapna *akka's*.

"And Aditi is a non-vegetarian, so she would have to stop cooking or eating non-veg in the house or maybe give it up altogether as we are vegetarians. And it will be such a crime for her to give up something that she has grown up eating."

I didn't respond, I was surprised at everything that she said, and the rationale provided, which sounded very shallow.

Radhika's was a love marriage. She met Amar, a Tamil Brahmin, when she worked at Synergy Finance. He was doing phenomenally well in his career. She fell in love with him, and broke the news to my parents. My dad was open minded and supportive, given Amar was an eligible bachelor and nothing concerning except that he hailed from a different community. As soon as they got married, Amar lost his job and fell into hard times. Five years had passed and he hadn't still found a job. Radhika resumed working and became the bread winner. I was extending a minor help in paying the monthly mortgage of their house that they had purchased after marriage.

There were similar episodes of love marriages that ended in major failure for different reasons with our other two distant cousins. The general sentiment was that love marriages were jinxed in our family, whatever be the reason.

Yet, I found it silly that my sister articulated this as a matter of concern. In all those instances, the marriages were impacted because of the guys who came from outside the community. Here, I was the guy! And, I wasn't seeking to marry any ordinary girl.

Aditi was someone that you just meet once in a lifetime; that is how I felt about her. Did she have any idea of what Aditi was like? Didn't the emails and her writing give a good sense of her.

Not to mention, Aditi being a non-vegetarian was of no consequence to me at all; it didn't matter. She could eat whatever she wanted.

I was truly surprised at Radhika's superficial assessment. Nor did she probe further into my feelings for her. Maybe she was caught in her own wrap of life's crises or maybe I wasn't forceful enough in expressing my feelings for Aditi with her.

Two weeks passed. I met my school friends, college mates, family members, spoke to uncles and aunts, my cousins and visited Tirupati.

I didn't call Aditi nor did I check my emails or write to her, during all that time. In my third week, when I returned from Tirupati, I rode my dad's scooter to an Internet café center and checked my emails on Friday evening.

There were a few emails from Aditi, where she mentioned that she had to travel to Mumbai for work, when her brother was visiting Delhi from US, and it was such a bummer. She was on a contract with the company, and hence was expected to travel, wherever they offered her a new assignment. Her new work entailed long duration stays in Mumbai in the future for weeks and months; and she was busy looking for a place to stay.

18 December 2000

Dear Aditi,

Hi! I am v v v sorry for the late reply. We had started for Tirupati last Mon morn and came back just today.

*It is very unfortunate that you must be in Bombay just around
the time your brother is in Delhi. He must be disappointed as
well.*

Did you fly back this weekend to see him?

*How is he doing? What did he get for you and your mom?
What's your current assignment in Bombay?*

*I know that it's going to be very difficult for you to put up
in Mumbai all alone. And I guess, staying alone in a small,
compact and hip city like Pune with a company paid mobile,
plenty of friends is very different from staying in a remote corner
of Mumbai, and with no friends. I hate it when I'm alone in my
flat – get that tinge of depression. But you'll manage, I'm certain.*

*I have booked my return tickets for 30th Dec. I'm reaching
Delhi on Monday the 1st around 9.40ish at night.*

*I have lots more to tell you, but wondering if I should talk to
you over the phone or mail you. Might as well send you another
mail.*

*But, otherwise, are you enjoying yourself in the office in
Bombay?*

Write in.
Shyam

20 December 2000

Hi!

*Good to know that you had a good trip. Would bear fruit. I am
unlucky not to have been able to make a pilgrimage yet. Too
many sins I suppose...*

*I am back in Delhi. I reached yesterday evening. I was in
Bombay to make HR policies. I was supposed to finish that by*

31st Dec but I worked like crazy and finished them on 18th eve and flew back on the 19th. Now they would be debated upon by the senior management team and I might need to go back to make final amendments a week or so later. Not too sure.

It's great to be with my bro. He has got me a car cd, chocolates (as you predicted), some tops and lots of CDs.

Life is okay otherwise. Nothing great. Bombay was good work wise but I was feeling too lonely.

Bye and take care
Aditi

21 December 2000

Dear Aditi,

Hi! Don't worry. Making a pilgrimage beginning of next year is a good idea. You can start the year afresh. It's just that you need to find someone for company. It happens. What could you do if you are summoned to Mumbai for some urgent work? Let your mom be with you till things take a definite shape. You need someone till then.

A family reunion is always a great feeling, specially to meet up with a US-returned brother. You must be happy with those beautiful tops and CDs. Are you all sitting tight inside the house or going outside? I normally don't when I go home for a short visit.

What are your parents suggesting to you about your work?

Take care.
Write in.
Shyam

21 December 2000

Hi!

As for fun, yes it is. Have been going out the last two evenings. My bro wanted to pick up some shirts and jackets, so did the driver's job. Have been here only three evenings so not a bad track record. Bro also has some travelling to do.

As for my parent's idea about my job; it is the same old Indian thinking. They want me to get married and get out of their hair. Surprisingly, my bro has joined the bandwagon.

The last leg of your holiday is almost begun. Make the most of it. You'll miss home when you are back. Enjoy yourself and come back all charged!

Bye and take care
Aditi

2.32

27 December 2000

Dear Aditi,

I have been having a throat pain for the last seven days. It's a very uneasy feeling. Might have to switch over to a stronger dose of antibiotics today.

Where did your brother travel to?

Aditi, before & during the vacation, I had been giving a serious thought to life, love & marriage. I don't possess the 'feel-good-factor' for marriage at this point. (Would blame it on my work.)

Nor does my financial position allow me to entertain such thoughts. Feel that the guy should have a min of five to ten lakhs cash in hand at the time of marriage, being told that a heart of gold is of no use without any kind of financial security. More importantly, my brother-in-law is passing through a rough phase (financially) and I was constantly thinking that it was just a matter of time before it got resolved, but after coming here, I understand that there have been no improvements.

In my last mail, I mentioned that I have lots to tell you. Well they were these disturbing thoughts. I couldn't wait to speak to you. In Tirupati and the other temples, all that I have been praying was for the attainment of a happy state of mind and a feel-good factor. It's truly sad that this is something that evades most of us.

It's Thursday evening. Will try to check my mailbox one more time before I leave. But in any case, let me wish you in advance: HAPPY NEW YEAR. Enjoy yourself and try to uncage at least on the 31st night; go out and have fun.

Take care.
Write in.
Shyam

I had dropped the bombshell. She made no reply.

2.33

I became restless and anxious to hear back from her. I went to the internet center a few times to check for her reply. There was none. On the day I had to take the train back to Delhi, I went in the morning again. None from her. It was the first time since we had gotten close to each other, there was no reply from her.

Expectedly, she must have been terribly shocked at what I wrote; jolted, to say the least. Yet, it was remarkable that she was so graceful about it and never confronted me directly at why I wrote that.

She did call me a few times when I reached Delhi; but the length of the conversations was short. In her first phone call, on the 2nd, she even enquired why I didn't call her as soon as I landed. I had no answer.

She didn't show anger or animosity with me, but stopped writing mails to me on her own. She however did respond when I wrote to her; although she now took days, if not a week to reply. Her replies were far shorter too.

I was starting to find it difficult to handle. I still desired her friendship, and still looked forward to her emails. The heart is such a beast. Now, as she started to walk away from me, my heart started to long for her more.

I wondered if I had acted hurriedly by writing an email from Coimbatore. I should have met her and told her what I was going through. Maybe she would have summarily dismissed my concerns, and plainly told me I was being stupid in being so hard on myself.

But I had created an irreparable gap with her with that e-mail. How would I explain to her the complex set of opposing feelings in an email or over the phone? Only in a face to face meeting could I hope to salvage our relation.

I had to meet her.

15 January 2001

Sub: I want to meet up & talk

Hi,

Sometimes in life, we might have seen or heard about say, two persons who are extremely pally with one another, placing complete trust in the relationship or are in love, and suddenly, one of them shows a deviation from the normal expected behaviour towards the other, inflicting a great deal of mental injury to the other in the process. While this is definitely wrong, the least the person could have done is to go forward and explain the reasons for the sudden shift in the behaviour rather than leaving the other struggling to wonder what went wrong.

Was just debating whether I should send this mail or not, but decided to go ahead because I fully trust you to handle this.

If by chance, you find all this crap and utter nonsense and say I'm imagining things, I will definitely not feel that I've made a fool of myself. Instead, as you finish reading the last line of this mail, I will have that small element of consolation that I have been honest to someone who has been a sweetheart to me.

We have come a long way since September 2000 and have seen it go a step beyond friendship. And somewhere midway through, our mails and conversation acquired the obvious undertone. Let me not deny this from my side and I'm sure you won't either. Stepping back, in this context, I know that the last mail that I wrote from Coimbatore must have sounded abrupt, causing shock, pain and hurt. I too felt churlish about it.

How do I continue now? It's difficult to put all these in words and so had requested for a meeting last weekend. Wanted to talk it over but at least I wanted to tell you this much so that I don't have the guilt pangs. In addition to the ones listed in the mail, more importantly, there is one more – I wonder if I will ever get an opportunity to meet up and talk to you.

Hope that I didn't complicate things further or embarrass you by writing this and trust we will keep this aside and continue talking. If you want to scold me, please do so.

Just wanted to say this much.

Shyam

She didn't reply. I waited for a few days and a week. There was no response from her. I wrote a casual email, without any reference to wanting to meet her; telling her briefly about work, and my weekend to which she did reply.

I wanted to call her, but it had become weird. Mental blocks were already in my mind. What would I say to her; or would she even entertain me. Yet, I tried calling her a few times at home and work. Her parents said she had gone out or I had disconnected the call hearing their voices.

22 February 2001

Re:

Hi!

Thanks for the mail. I had called up your number 6841975 today morning around 11ish and was told by the guard that you have not arrived in the office yet. Please let me know at which number I can reach you.

Shyam

22 February 2001

Hi!

How have you been? I landed in Delhi finally. Tried calling you up a hundred times today. Now we have an EPABX so getting 'O' as such is quite a job.

I have been busy catching up with pending work (whatever little has accumulated in past 3 weeks) and trying to streamline everything. Might be back in Bombay next week so have lots to do.

My Watson Wyatt comp survey is going fine. I need to finally cap the HR Practices survey that I did in December.

Rest the same.
Aditi

After multiple attempts that day, I could finally reach her at work. As soon she heard my voice, she merely said, 'I will call you back' and ended the call abruptly before I could speak a word. Five days later, she did the same.

27 February 2001

Dear Aditi,

Well, this is the second time that the call had to end abruptly. If it had been someone, the first time would have been the last time.

I would not have disturbed the person again at all. But in your case, I can't let it go. I'm not at all complaining or being touchy but just being sensitive enough to understand that you actually don't want to be called. Okay, will not do so in future.

This call was perhaps one more attempt of mine to put the missing link in our relationship.

Our last meeting was in April 2000 and when we met, it was under different circumstances and in the past few months, I always thought it was important for me to meet you at least a couple of times before I...

Anyway, there is no point in elaborating all that now. Don't know what to say. And also, unsure if I'm doing the right thing by sending this mail to you.

I am just sorry for the whole thing.

Take care and do well.
Shyam

27 February 2001

Hi!

I appreciate your being so upfront and honest about the way you feel but somehow, I can't handle complex relationships/ feelings. I'm a little conservative in my approach and go by things which are well thought out/accepted and acceptable.

I haven't been on this trip ever and I find it difficult to handle. I look at life differently, but for me, not all things are as they appear.

I'm sorry for being rude and curt.

I think we can always keep in touch. Don't see any hassle in a normal, no-feelings kind of a thing. Up to you.

All the best to you too,

Aditi

27 February 2001

Dear Aditi,

I'm very sorry for the delayed reply. It is 10:30 p.m. now and I wanted to stay back and write to you in peace. I feel that there is a gap in what I said in those mails and what you could have interpreted.

Yes, I was wrong to send you mail from Coimbatore. I should have simply talked to you. That would have eliminated these disconnects. Looks like the email is not an effective medium to address this.

It's in such situations of 'love', I really wish I could think through the heart. Things would be much easier to decide. Is it a Cancerian trait to think through the mind? It just doesn't help under these circumstances.

When I read this line, 'I haven't been on this trip ever and I find it difficult to handle', it makes me feel worse. I have realized that the three things that I had listed – feel good factor, money and my brother-in-law's financial condition – all the three are inevitable and I have reconciled to that.

Aditi, you can help me by listening to me. Allow me to speak to you at least over the phone. Let's have a heart to heart talk where I tell you about my complete thought process, I will be absolutely frank with you and you will promise to tell me whatever you feel on my face.

If you ask me, what exact purpose would this call or meeting serve? I don't have a definite answer. I just strongly feel that we should. Please respond. We can do this once you are back from Bombay – this weekend. Even if you are not willing to meet me, please tell me a time as to when you can call at my home. Please.

Take care and write in.
Shyam

She didn't reply to this email specifically, but kept responding to my other casual emails, at her own pace.

I felt terrible. The more silent and distant she had become, my heart longed for her more and more. I repented my mistake. I wanted her back in my life. I wanted to marry her. She was my wholesome beauty, a divine beauty – a person with a noble heart and a beautiful mind. She was someone who liked, and respected me for what I was; someone who teased me and laughed at my imperfections and stupidity. With her, life would be a celebration. Pure Bliss.

One day, I wrote an email to her, filled with emotions and hope, asking her the sacred four words that had been just unthinkable a few months ago.

8 March 2001

Dear Aditi,

I have been just thinking of you and the feeling has only increased in these past months.

I'm asking you – will you marry me?

Today is Wednesday and I'm hoping to hear from you by Friday evening. And in case I don't see any mail from you by then, I will assume it as a 'Yes'. Next, on Saturday morning, I will be talking to my parents about this.

In addition to all that you know about me, I also meet your three conditions.

I'm not a doctor.

I don't wear glasses.

I'm definitely taller than you.

Please say 'yes'.

I have lots to tell you but do not know how to say it. Aditi, you know me well. Make a fair judgement and decide.

Write in. Am waiting eagerly, and anxiously for your mail.

Love,
Shyam

After sending the email, I was nervously checking my mail box every few minutes. Few hours passed. It was past 5:30 p.m. She normally left work at 5:30. Probably she would reply tomorrow, I thought.

Along with the nervousness and the trembling fear, I had a strange feeling of goodness that I asked her finally and said those words that were deep in my heart, uncaring for my mind.

Out of blue, I saw a reply from her pop up in my mail box.

8 March 2001

Hi,

I don't think you should wait till Friday. Please close the chapter here. I'm not into this anymore.

Bye,
Aditi

Four months later, in July, she merely emailed me her wedding invitation. The wedding was in Bangalore with a Telugu guy.

I was crushed.

What kind of god would let me meet someone so beautiful, earn her love, make me fall in love in the unlikeliest of circumstances, and yet, let me screw it all up?

Two Big Revelations of Life:

The Mind and the Heart are such beasts; that they tend to have furiously opposing thoughts sometimes.

When I should have gone by my heart, I listened to the sounds of my mind. I should have never said a 'no' to Aditi.

And when I should have gone by my mind; I listened to the beats of my heart, succumbing to the emotional pressure. I should have never said a 'yes' to Padma.

My dad died a year later, after my annulment in 2004. He was heart-broken at my steadfast refusal to live with Padma; it had caused him enormous grief. He had felt very sorry and personally responsible for Padma and her parents, and had taken it as his crusade in getting me back with her. He was just fifty-five years old when he passed away.

A few years after after his demise, during one of my India trips, I had shared with Radhika for the first time about my irrational fear in select speaking situations at work. She took me to a well-known and respected psychiatrist in Bangalore.

He listened to my symptoms patiently, and kept nodding his head as I described at length of that incident that sparked it; and its inconsistency in manifestation – that it appeared to be limited to some work situations, not all. I explained as best as I could, the physiological symptoms that accompanied it and the morbid thought of the prospect of my voice failing, and being unable to speak a word at my speaking turn.

I was even surprised at his ready nods that signaled understanding; but what the heck. Was he offering fake empathy? How in the world can anyone show such a ready display of easy understanding what I had gone through?

After he heard me out, he calmly asked, "Is there anything you want to add more or say, before I give you my diagnosis of your condition."

I said, "No."

He emphatically said that my condition was caused by a deficiency in serotonin levels in the brain.

The serotonins are the happy hormones, and when there is a deficiency, it causes anxiety, bordering on irrationality depending on the magnitude of deficiency. He gave it a term, 'social anxiety', and talked on fight and flight response, and beta blockers. People with excessively high serotonin levels tend to be high risk takers, which could be good or bad by themselves. Good as in those folks who experience high adrenalin rush, and want to do daring sports and find joy in it, as an example. Bad, as in, that it is not uncommon to find higher serotonin levels in criminals, propelling them to be risk takers.

He said, "Speaking situations that are otherwise easy and comfortable for an average person with an average serotonin level is very stressful and anxiety inducing for the person with a deficiency in the same situation.

"I will prescribe you an anti-anxiety medicine. Start with a 25 gms dosage daily. After two weeks, give me a call, and let's see how you feel. Based on that, I will alter the dosage, reduce or increase it slightly. You will be fine from now on.

"This is just a band-aid. The long-term cure is meditation. I will encourage you to meditate daily. Meditation calms the mind and the nerves. That is the only permanent cure."

This was a huge revealing moment in my life. I was plain stumped.

Had I known this much before, maybe I would not have beaten myself down to the extent I did, by being so hard and critical of myself in viewing it as a personal inadequacy, and instead may have been comfortable and at ease in revealing everything to Aditi without much fear of being judged as being weak. And who knows, she would have shrugged it of no consequence and chided me for being silly in thinking of staking away our future together due to this. And that was all I would have needed to move forward, and asked her the sacred four words.

Overnight, the quality of my life had increased tremendously, since I started taking the pills. It had not erased the anxiety completely; but it helped me to get back to leading closer to a normal life. I had never fathomed there was a band-aid in the form of a medicine for this condition. This was my first revelation.

Knowing that there are no short-cuts in life for happiness, success or cure, I believed the medicines were meant only as a band-aid; and not form a dependence on it permanently.

The second revelation.

I had a misguided belief all along that our lives were pre-destined, and what was meant to happen was bound to happen. At several instances with Aditi, when I was trying to seek a meeting with her, or talk to her after I returned from Coimbatore, I was subconsciously aware that the efforts that I had put in to get back with her, were partial. And when my partial efforts didn't generate the desired outcome, I had stopped myself from continuing in my efforts, and gave up in despair, telling myself that I had done my bit, and if it was meant to happen, it would happen surely.

Nothing is more wrong than that. Because, what I had not truly understood then, was I had short-changed in my efforts. I had NOT given my very best, my one hundred percent. And then and there, I had erred greatly on the very spiritual foundation of life, that you put in your efforts, and give it one hundred percent. Simple, nothing less. That is life's Dharma, which I had not known then, and had not followed.

Probably, the outcome may have been different if I had given my hundred percent.

Karmay-evaadhikaaraste maa phaleshu kadaachana
Maa karmaphalaheturbhuurmaa te sango.astvakarmani'

The right is to work only; but never to its fruit; Let not the fruit of action be thy motive, nor let thy attachment be to inaction.

– *(Bhagavad Gita,* chapter 2; verse 47*)*

That is one part of the right understanding, and attitude to have.

I had met a saint at his ashram in the outskirts of Bangalore. He said, "Your height is your Karma; your weight is your Free will. Life is not all Destiny, it is a combination of Free Will and Destiny." And gave an example, "When it is raining outside, that is destiny; going out with an umbrella, or getting wet is your free will..."

It is only then that I realized that you have enough latitude on free-will. You should not limit yourself, and your life, into subscribing that everything is pre-destined, and be fatalistic and refrain from putting your sincere, complete efforts.

Only when the desired outcome does not occur, despite all your very best efforts, do you then, let go, and accept the results. It is here, you bring in the notion of destiny or Karma, for the wise thing to do is to tell yourself it was pre-destined and not meant to be, and thus nullify any accompanying regret of the outcome. And there will be no regrets of not having done enough either. You tell yourself, that whatever happens is for the very best; and better things await in your life.

The saint succinctly summarized it, "Your Past is your Destiny. Your Future is your Free Will. Your Present is your *Prarabdha Karma.*"

If you don't strive; nothing will yield to you. The future is a blank canvas, symbolizing that you have the potential power to create any greater possibilities out of it.

What else may explain why I was handed this serotonin imbalance and to lead a very torturous life during a crucial phase of my life?

Why did my dad's time come?

Was I really meant to marry Shrisha, and had to go through all this drama just to finally meet her?

Why did I meet Aditi? If that holy union of matrimony was not destined between us. Why all that drama and heartbreak?

Why did Padma meet me? If there was no way she could have me in her life.

Why all that drama and heartbreak for her?

We were all meant to have these life experiences; propelled from our past actions; following the laws of nature and cosmic force; for that is the *niyati.*

All the pain and trauma I underwent resulted from my own actions done in past life-times? Maybe we all had some life lessons to learn.

The only way I could reconcile with all these unpleasant events was believing, that all that happened was driven by Karma. It was destined that way. It lightens up the burden of the painful past.

I have moved on. I have come to believe this is how it was meant to be. My story had to play out only this way. There are a lot of interconnected events that it is hard to imagine that it could have played any other way.

Ah, life is such a hologram! The same events offer a completely different perspective, when looked at it, in different time periods.

But understand that when it comes to my future, I have all free-will, not limited by Karma, and think and act like that.

Like for example, this crazy endeavor of mine in believing that I would get this book published.

If I think life had handed me lemons, I might as well try making sweet lemonade out of it! As much as a cliché as it sounds, there is nothing better that succinctly reflects this sentiment.

Make the best use of the cards that Life has dealt you with! If it is the Joker, go fully for it and play out the game to your very best!

Fast Forward

Padma has re-married and has two kids, I recently learnt. I believe she lives in the US.

Though I had wronged her and her family, they had been very noble; and didn't do anything to harm or hurt me. All that I write here is obviously from my perspective; Padma may have a different story to tell.

Aditi has a daughter who is in her teens now. And when she was born, she did share the news with me saying, 'Riya does not know you, yet. :)'. I was trading occasional emails with her until 2006, after which, I have not made any attempt to write to her.

Shrisha and I have a son.

But to get here, I had to go through so much of drama.

Unfathomable are the ways of Karma.

Epilogue

1 June 2005

Hi Aditi,

I am sorry for sending in an abrupt mail like this. And you may wonder as to why I should be doing it now. And what I tell you would be of absolute unconcern for you now, for things change and we move on with life.

Over the years, I had always wanted to seek an opportunity to explain and tell you the complete truth. Just for the simple reason that I don't want it to remain a mystery or an unsolved puzzle that had deeply bruised your mind, heart and soul in the past.

Of course, I am putting myself in your shoes and hence writing this mail. For I would have never been able to reconcile with a person if someone had done a similar thing to me and would have felt hurt beyond words if the person didn't even offer to tell the real truth as to why she was stepping out of the relationship. I would have never been able to understand a person like that and would have found it unmanageable to contain a sense of anger, outrage, pain and hurt.

I will make it real brief. While I just said that 'I don't have a feel-good factor for marriage', what I left unsaid was the reason behind it. I was in a state of depression that was so severe because of 'something'. And that 'something' is beyond your comprehension or anyone else's guess. The trauma (mildly put) that I went through affected my psyche and my sense of self-worth. And you must be in total disbelief for you had no inkling of it in my numerous emails or in the phone conversations.

My family too was shocked when they heard about it later from me. Someday, I will tell you what that 'something' is, if you really want to know.

With this, I rest my case. I am not sure if I've made any sense.

Would really appreciate if you mail me back.

Regards to your husband, love to Riya, and pranams to your parents,

Shyam

8 June 2005

Hi Shyam,

Relax. It's nice to know that the reasons were genuine. Don't worry about it anymore.

Aditi

It is when I saw this reply from Aditi, did I lose the original motivation to write further on my incomplete story. Time had healed the terrible hurt I had caused to her.

Fast Forward Again

I was heading back to the US from London. At the time of boarding the flight, I requested the agent at the gate for an aisle seat. He smiled back and said he was assigning me in a row with all the three seats empty. I thanked him and was so glad that I could lie down, and sleep.

But just before the take-off, a lady seated in the middle of four seats, right across me in the front row came over to my row to take up the window seat. I was initially bummed that I would no longer be able to lie down and relax!

Samantha Lurrel broke the ice, and she said she is part of Access Consciousness. That got me talking merrily with her! She said their belief is – *you ask and you will receive it*, which reminded me of Paulo Coelho's, 'if you desire something deeply with all your heart, the entire Universe will conspire to provide it to you.'

I had an amazing chat with her. I shared with her my irrational anxiety and she said some deep things referring to it and past life regressions, that set me wondering. She asked me to say out a number instantly without thinking to how many times I was killed in my prior life-times. I said twelve. She said, "No wonder, you have experienced this anxiety to this intensity. Twelve times, you have been murdered for speaking out your mind, and in saying what you felt."

She chanted a prayer and smilingly said, "This should go away now."

I was left wondering, that me bumping into her was not a random occurrence. She and I never sat in our original assigned seats, but moved around only to meet up in this manner.

❖

Depression is a Disease of Civilization:
Hunter-Gatherers Hold the Key to theCure

It robs people of sleep, energy, focus, memory, sex drive and their basic ability to experience the pleasures of life, says author of *The Depression Cure,* Stephen Ildari. It can destroy people's desire to love, work, play and even their will to live. If left unchecked, it can cause permanent brain damage.

Depression lights up the pain circuitry of the brain to such an extent that many of Ildari's psychiatric patients have called it torment, agony and torture. "Many begin to look to death as a welcome means of escape," he said in a Ted Talks presentation.

But depression is not a natural disease. It is not an inevitable part of being human. Ildari argues, like many diseases, depression is a disease of civilization. It's a disease caused by a high stress, industrialized, modern lifestyle that is incompatible with our genetic evolution.

Depression is the result of a prolonged stress-response, Ildari said. The brain's "runaway stress response" – as he calls it – is similar to the fight or flight response, which evolved to help our ancestors when they faced predators or other physical dangers. The runaway stress response required intense physical activity for a few seconds, a few minutes, or – in extreme cases – a few hours.

"The problem is for many people throughout the Western world, the stress response goes on for weeks, months and even years at a time, and when it does, it's incredibly toxic," Ildari said.

Living under continually stressful conditions – as many modern humans do – is disruptive to neuro-chemicals like dopamine and serotonin, which can lead to sleep disturbance, brain damage, immune dysregulation and inflammation, Ildari says.

(Published in Mar'16)
By Sara Burrows at filmsforaction.org